Rhiar

A Welsh Island Story

by

Roscoe Howells

Gomer Press
1987

First Impression/1987

ISBN 0 86383 379 9

© Roscoe Howells

Printed by Gomer Press, Llandysul, Dyfed

For

ALEX and DONNIE

In gratitude for friendship and encouragement

Contents

Prologue

The fisherman was old now. His blue eyes retained their brightness, but his hair was white and his step was slower.

His garden was still tidy and well kept, scarcely ever without vegetables, and always with an abundance of flowers in season. But only rarely these days did he put to sea, although he could not bring himself to part with his old boat. His had been the last boat to fish from the village.

Nor, for a long time, had he visited The Island. It was all in the past, and soon to be forgotten.

That was the sad part. Everything would be forgotten. Long years ago his young wife had died with their first child, so he was the last of the family. And family had always been so important.

Maybe it did not matter so much about the puffins, but it was sad even so. Time was when he could remember great numbers of puffins coming to The Island to breed and, long before that, so it had been said in the old stories handed down in the family, they used to come in their countless thousands. Nowadays there was scarcely a puffin to be seen.

He lacked for nothing, but had few possessions. His cottage was trim, and clean and comfortable.

All that he had of value, which he treasured beyond price, was the bracelet.

Bronze it was, and finely wrought. Penannular and burnished, it was toothed and of exquisite workmanship. Nor had it any dark green patina, but retained its original rich bronze lustre.

In the family it was said to have been handed down to succeeding generations since time began. How long exactly, nobody could rightly say. But, after the manner of those who lived in remote and isolated communities, they passed on many stories to those who came after them, and they were a people rich in culture.

When the bird-ringers could get their hands on a puffin they would put a ring on its leg. Soon, by the look of things, there would be no more puffins left to ring.

Nor would there be anybody left to wear the bracelet, or treasure it, or to hear the stories of those to whom it had belonged in other days.

Somebody would put a cash value on the bracelet. But nobody cared about family or heritage.

Chapter 1

The Past

(1)

It had been a hard winter for the puffin. For week after week the storms had driven him across the endless expanse of ocean until at times he felt he would not be able to go on. When he took to the air for a brief respite from the buffeting of the mountainous waves he found himself being swept along helplessly by the fury of the wind. And then, as his strength ebbed away, he saw a great something, he knew not what, and he flutttered over it, his short clockwork wings beating like a hovering moth, and eased himself down on to this place of rest and safety, rolling about in the immensity of the storm-ridden seas.

The tree-trunk had been hollowed out for almost its whole length, but, although the crude vessel was full of water, it still floated and a small area of its surface was not quite submerged. Almost before the puffin had settled he was joined by another one, and then another, until eventually more than a score of them were riding out the storm together.

Whenever a great wave broke over them, carrying them away with it, they would swim, sometimes on top of the water, and sometimes under it as their wings and their orange coloured web feet drove them forward, before fluttering back onto the raft. Then, at last, after many days, the storm suddenly blew itself out and the puffin dropped back into the water and began diving in search of the small fish which were its food.

The whole little party remained fairly close together as they fished and then sported above the waves, but one of the puffins remained closer to him than any of the others. Presently he rubbed his great, hooked and brightly coloured beak against hers and she croaked with pleasure. The winter moult was over and he flapped his wings in excitement and displayed his new and shining plumage, black on his back and white in front.

The days of storm and dark skies were followed by warm
sunshine and the puffin sensed in the others the excitement
he was experiencing himself. For eight months they had
lived far out of sight of land upon the vastness of the ocean
where other sea-birds were their only companions and
where there were no enemies and little danger. Now the
puffin knew a great desire and there was a sense of urgency
to reach land.

He knew the place well. He had been born there and for
some years had been returning in the spring to find a mate.
Blown far off course by the storm he yet knew the direction
he should take, and each day, as he journeyed ever land-
wards with his companions, the excitement became more
intense.

The Island was a good place and sea-birds beyond number
came there in the summer-time to breed. Here were hardly
any more enemies than on the water. Peregrine falcons
which had their eyries in the high crags of the great cliff
would swoop to strike the unwary with their talons in mid-
air. It meant instant death when the falcon struck. But there
were not so many of them because there was little food for
them on The Island through the winter. The buzzards, too,
and the ravens and crows would sometimes kill the weak or
sickly but the worst enemies were the gulls. And, the great
black-backed gulls were the most vicious. In the water they
would attack, hunting slyly in pairs, or waiting patiently for
long periods at the entrance to the puffins's nest, deep down
in a burrow, to spear with their cruel beaks as the puffin
emerged.

There were not many gulls because, like the falcons, they
found little food on The Island or anywhere nearby during
the winter, but the other sea-birds were there now in
myriads. Ledge upon ledge was packed every summer with
the razorbills and guillemots, whilst the puffins and shearwaters thronged the breeding burrows. There were storm
petrels too.

The Island had been a good place for breeding in all the
years the puffin had been coming there. Every year the grass

grew up and died back and left a thick mat in which it was
easy to burrow deep down into the darkness to make a cosy
chamber where his mate could lay her large white egg. The
cliff-tops were honeycombed with these burrows. Sometimes the puffin found it necessary to dispute possession
with a shearwater, but the fight was never serious and there
was room for all. But whereas the shearwaters emerged only
by night, the puffins by day covered the cliff-tops like
thousands of daisies, or swam in huge flocks with the razorbills and guillemots where the ocean lifted and fell at the foot
of the cliffs.

Each day now the puffin saw that his own little flock had
been joined by others and at sunset on the day he sighted
The Island there were many thousands gathered upon the
water. Next day they moved in close ready to repossess
their breeding quarters. It was good to be back.

On the sea, in the air, and on the ledges of the cliff above
them, sea-birds beyond number groaned and screamed as
they jostled for position or called to their mates. Everywhere
was great stir and bustle.

Two days later the puffin took to the air for an exploratory
flight above the cliff-tops to seek out a burrow for his mate.
As he circled he saw movement. They were strange
creatures, bigger, far bigger, than any bird he had seen
before, but they made no attempt to fly. Never in all his life
had he seen such creatures as these.

Eventually he settled on the turf and, head on one side
with curiosity, allowed one of these strange creatures to
approach quite close before he fluttered back down to the
sea.

The puffin could not know it or understand, but man had
come.

(2)

Although it had been a hard winter for the puffin, it had
also been a hard winter for the man.

For years his tribe had been declining in numbers as they
retreated ever westwards before the onslaughts of the

advancing Celts. Always they took with them what livestock they could, but always they lost the homes they had built and the land they had struggled to cultivate.

Now, at last, they had reached the peninsula, and his own small group had become separated from the main tribe. They could go no further.

Fortunately, some who had joined the group had come from one of the tribes of boatbuilders. Throughout the previous summer the man had set them to building boats. Some were skin-covered and some were canoes, fashioned roughly from hollowed-out tree trunks. Whilst the boatbuilders worked, the man set others to raising stone fortifications to hold the peninsula as long as they could. He knew that their only hope now, faint though it was, was to reach The Island beyond.

During the siege he sometimes stood on the cliff-top and studied the winds and the fierce currents between the peninsula and The Island. When spring came, and their food was running low, they loaded all their trussed livestock into their frail boats, and set off on their short but perilous voyage. Not all of them reached their destination. Those who did were fortunate to find a place to serve as a track to the cliff-top.

The man saw that The Island was a good place. Immediately he set the group to work again raising stone fortifications at the top of the track. It should be an easy place to hold.

No trees grew upon The Island but there was much grass, springs of fresh water and, on a small area of moor, they found peat to burn.

The man, however, had much to occupy his mind. It would be a long time, he knew, before their livestock could breed, and they dare not kill them for food now. Nor could they expect a quick return from the land they tilled. But when they had been there only a few weeks, the birds came and the man set some of the young men to work erecting a circle of stones as a tribute to the god who had sent this source of food.

The eggs of all the birds were good, but the people soon discovered that the puffins were the easiest birds to catch as they emerged from their nesting burrows. Their flesh was good and the oil from them could be stored in stone containers. Later, when the young arrived and were ready to flutter and tumble down to the sea, they were found to be even plumper and more tasty than the older birds.

In the autumn, when the birds had gone, the seals came to breed in the caves and on the pebbly beaches, and the man set his little group to clubbing them to death, using their pelts and rendering down the fat for use in the winter. By that time they had built their first huts of stone and roofed them with turf and rush. In extremity, they found that the meat of the seals was good to eat.

Hard though their first winter on The Island was, it was much better than they had experienced the previous year during the siege on the peninsula. Although there was no wood they were able to burn the oil from the birds and the seals for heating. But how long such a satisfactory state of affairs could last the man was not sure.

It was on a warm day during the second springtime, when the birds had returned, and the men and women, old and young, were busy collecting eggs from the more accessible ledges, that a boy who had been left to keep watch on the cliff-top, came running.

'Tad! Tad!' he was shouting. 'They come.'

(3)

In bigger, stronger skin-covered boats, the invaders were coming. They had had more than a year in which to build them whilst they settled on the peninsula abandoned by the small tribe in their flight westward to The Island.

Of the Brythonic strain of Celts these newcomers were, of the tribe of the Demetae, short and dark like the Silures, their allies. And though most of their weapons were of flint and bronze, like those which had been used for hundreds of years, they also had weapons of iron similar to those now in use amongst the tribes further to the east.

The first of the Celts to attempt the cliff track were met by a volley of stones.

The young chief had hair on his face and down to his shoulders. He had been sent by his father on this venture and saw no need to hurry. Calling his men back, he kept some at the foot of the track to occupy the attention of the defenders, and sent others in their boats to skirt the island in search of places where the cliffs were less high and easier to climb. Long before the sun was sinking below the wide horizon, way out beyond the sea, the last remnants of the ancient tribe of stone men in the far west had been surrounded and overpowered by the more numerous Celts.

The young chief ordered chains to be fastened round the necks of the captives, men and women and children, in groups of five, ready to take them back to the peninsula and then to the Big Harbour where they could be shipped as slaves. There was one maiden, however, tall and more comely than any the young man had ever seen. He gazed long into her eyes, and defiantly she stared back at him.

She was not put in chains. He had decided to keep her for himself. She would be his queen, and so he called her Rigantona.

(4)

Rigantona was one of the oldest names known to the early Celtic people, and the young chief thought it would be a good name for the beautiful girl he had taken as his wife.

Two identical bracelets he had. One he gave to Rigantona and one he wore himself. Of finely wrought bronze they were, penannular and burnished, toothed and of exquisite workmanship, with a rich lustre.

Although the young chief and his people had come to The Island only in pursuit of the last remnant of the ancient tribe of stone men, having disposed of them, they found The Island to be a place fairer and more bountiful than anything they had imagined. The young chief remained with Rigantona and some of his followers. Rigantona spent the rest of her life on The Island and her children were born and lived there.

The young chief, however, had soon realised that it would be foolish to take the sea-birds indiscriminately and he had laid down strict rules for their exploitation, and had ensured that not too many were taken in any one season.

Near the cliff-tops, where the puffins nested, land was apportioned between different families where the puffins could be taken, and the people soon learned how to take the birds more easily. There was no shortage of water and, on the cliff-tops, where the streamlets fell down to the sea, huts were built where the carcasses were washed, dried and stored.

The more fertile land, where livestock was reared and crops grown, was also apportioned between the families. It was a good life. So numerous did the people become, and so great was the demand for land, that, by means of lynchets, they even made little fields so that they could cultivate the land which sloped down to the cliffs.

One stream was used to construct a series of seven ponds and here fish were cultivated, the bigger fish being moved on to the next pond in each stage of their growth until they were fit to be taken for food.

After the original settlement, however, it was found that, as the livestock increased in numbers, the cattle and sheep trampled down the long grass in which the puffins had always burrowed so early, and it became more difficult for the birds to find suitable nesting places. But their value was so great that the rules of good husbandry were rigorously applied and every effort was made to make things as easy as possible for them. As a result, there was always a satisfactory harvest of carcasses, many of which were traded to the mainland in return for other goods.

So it was that, for three centuries, the descendants of the tribe, whose first young chief had taken Rigantona for his wife, remained on The Island and prospered.

Even the coming of the Romans to the mainland meant nothing to them.

(5)

Whereas the presence of the Romans on the mainland had ensured many years of peace and prosperous trading, they had not had any other very great influence on the way of life of the people who lived on The Island, or indeed on any of the other tribes in the remote hill areas. Sometimes those members of the tribe who went to the mainland to trade brought back strange stories of Roman soldiers who spoke of someone they called Jesus Christ who, they said, had been crucified and had actually risen from the dead. More and more people, it seemed, were believing these stories and starting a new religion. They were called Christians. The Islanders, however, were content to worship their own gods who had brought the sea-birds back year after year as a source of food and livelihood.

They had been good years, too. Careful control of the taking of the birds and their eggs had brought its own just reward and there was no reason why such a satisfactory state of affairs should not have continued.

The trouble had begun the previous year and the Islanders were afraid of the consequences if there should be any repetition. A heathen tribe from Ireland had been allowed by the Romans to settle on the mainland. It had not been long before they learned of the rich sea-bird harvest taken on The Island each summer, and the previous year some of them had come to see for themselves. They had been few in number and the Islanders had been able to send them away. A few days later, however, they had returned, this time in great numbers, and the Islanders had been powerless to resist. For many years they had lived at peace, they had no weapons and they were outnumbered.

For week after week the Irish had stayed and taken the puffins. Now, in the springtime, when the puffins returned, the Irish returned too. The Islanders pleaded with them in vain.

The following year there were so few puffins that the Irish did not stay more than a week or so. But there were no puffins for the Islanders either, for the Irish had paid no heed to the

long established customs of the Islanders and had slaughtered indiscriminately. With an important source of their
winter food supply gone, and little left with which to trade
with the mainland, most of the Islanders moved to the
mainland to live.

(6)

All round the cliff-tops there were hutments and walls of
stone, and the creatures which did not fly spent much time
near the burrows, waiting for the puffins to emerge, and
sometimes even setting other smaller creatures to digging
into the burrows and chasing the puffins out. It was all very
worrying and dangerous.

The puffin had seen hundreds of others being caught by the
neck, by means of a long stick and a hair-noose, never to be
seen again, and getting into and out of the nesting burrow
had become a matter for extreme caution.

For some days now he had been at sea feeding, and it was
time to return to the nest to sit on the egg and allow his mate a
few days rest so that she, too, could feed and stretch her
wings. It should not be too long before the chick broke
through the shell and then both he and his mate would spend
time at sea in turn bringing back the small fish to feed the
young one.

There was no sign of danger as he swept up over the cliff-
top and, coming in against the breeze, landed on the sward
amongst the thrift, the pink of which both contrasted and
blended so well with his own bright colouring. He took a
quick look round and then scuttled down the tunnel into the
darkness.

He saw the white egg in the dark, but there was no sign of
his mate, which was unusual. She had always, until now,
waited for him to return before going off the nest herself. In
the darkness he explored the labrynth of which their own
nesting place formed a part. A few sitting puffins made
noises at him, not altogether unfriendly, and a shearwater
pecked at him, but there was no sign of his mate. He went out
onto the grass into daylight and looked around again, very

anxious now. Other puffins nodded and bobbed towards him but he returned to the egg. When he settled on it he sensed that it was cold.

Immediately he felt this coldness some instinct told him that it would be no use sitting on it further. Yet for several days, for long periods, he would sit on the egg, then go outside, fly down to the sea, swim and dive, then come back and stretch his wings on the cliff-top before sitting on the egg again.

Never again did he see his mate, however, and at last he gave up hope, and left the egg, and returned to the sea ready for another winter.

(7)

Although following the ravages of the heathen tribe from Ireland, most of the Islanders had left, there were some who remained, and their descendants continued to live on The Island for another five centuries. They grew a little barley to make bread, and lived on goats' milk, cheese and some meat, taking what sea-birds and eggs they could in the springtime.

With the decline of the Roman Empire the Roman soldiers were recalled and, on the mainland, the tribes once more began to fight amongst themselves. But there was nothing on The Island to attract them and, even when the Saxons came, the Islanders were left in peace.

Sometimes, especially when food was scarce, a whole family would move away to the mainland, but always some of the Islanders would stay.

After all these centuries, however, there was now only one of the bronze bracelets remaining. And it continued to be handed down from one generation to another.

(8)

The girl's name was Rhiannon. With a maturity beyond her years, full-bosomed and dark-eyed, she was beautiful to look upon. Shapely and clean of limb, she spent much time tending the sheep and roving the cliff-tops. In the springtime she picked the wild flowers and loved to see the birds return. She knew the stories, too, of how in years gone by the sea-birds with their large beaks used to come to The Island in their countless thousands until the Irish tribe had almost exterminated them in two summers of madness.

On her wrist she wore a bracelet of bronze. It had been handed down in her family through many generations and it was said that they were direct descendants of the chief to whom it had once belonged and who had remained on The Island with a small following when the ravages of the Irish had caused most of the tribe to remove to the mainland.

The old monk too, knew much of the story.

Far out on The Island he had his stone hut, growing vegetables but eating little. Every day, summer and winter, long before dawn he would be at prayer and, as he grew older, he seemed to spend more and more time in his devotions.

Rhiannon was the only one to whom he talked very much. For a long time now she had taken milk to him each day from her father's goats, and sometimes cheese and butter, and a little bread, made from the barley which they grew. And each day the old monk talked to her and told her something of the story of her people and of Jesus Christ. As she grew older she wanted to hear more and more about this Jesus.

After the killing of the birds by the Irish heathens, the old monk said, he did not think that many people would have lived on The Island. Then, at last, the great Roman Empire had begun to decay, the Roman soldiers had been recalled from Britain and the ancient tribes had once again begun to fight amongst themselves. It was in the years following on this, he said, that monks and saints had gone through the land teaching the people and telling them of Jesus.

Then the Saxons had come and taken much of the land. Now, he said, there was danger from the Black Pagans, known as Vikings.

From the North lands they came, sailing round the coast in long, shallow vessels, each driven by a square black sail and rows of oars, and with shields of black and yellow ranged alongside the bulwarks. They came to rob and ravage, to pillage and rape, to enslave and kill, burning down homes and churches, hating Jesus and worshipping pagan gods such as Odin and Thor. In Ireland they had already made settlements and were carrying out some of their raids from there.

(9)

Only four families lived on The Island now. As far as anyone knew from the stories handed down, life for many, many years had been much the same. They had their cattle, sheep and goats, from the carcasses of which they dried meat for the winter. They made cheese and butter, used the skins of the animals and spun wool to make garments. There was never much frost or snow and those animals which were not killed for food usually managed to find enough grazing to survive the winter. Bracken was cut in the autumn and used for bedding, both for man and beast, during the winter. Feathers from the puffins were also used, but there were not so many of these birds now coming to The Island to breed and they still had to be taken sparingly.

The eligugs and blackbirds, however, still came to the ledges every year in their hundreds of thousands and, although these sea-birds could not be caught, many of the ledges were sufficiently accessible for their eggs to be taken.

There were the seals, too. Each year, when summer was passing to autumn, the seals, which were often to be seen basking on the rocks or swimming and diving in the clear water, would come to the pebbly beaches and the dark caves to breed. Rhiannon loved to watch them and would stroke the baby seals with their coats of white fur in those few weeks before they took to the water. Often she had been into the caves where the young ones were. There was one big cave, bigger than all the others, which ran far back under The Island, and once she and her older brother had been trapped in there by the incoming tide. But he had laughed at her fears and led her up onto a high ledge above the level of the water and there they had sat in the darkness until the sea had gone back.

Many seals came to breed in this big cave and it was at this time of year that the men killed them for their skins and fat, as well as for their flesh which was dried. Sometimes seal-skins were taken to the mainland to barter for other goods, but for many years there had not been very much trading, and life on The Island was self-contained and uneventful.

For the last year or two this peace had been disturbed by the presence of the Vikings' longboats round the coast, and the sight of them aroused fear amongst those who lived on The Island. For one whole summer there had been no sign of them at all and then, the following spring, shortly after the birds returned, there had been more of the boats to be seen than ever before.

It was a hot, dry summer and almost every day smoke could be seen rising on the mainland as homesteads were burned to the ground. The horrors the people were suffering did not bear thinking about and the old monk spent nearly all his time in prayer. Throughout the summer this continued and then one day, when the birds had gone and the seals had again started breeding, a boy, who had been watching from the cliff-top, came running.

'Tad! Tad!' he was shouting. 'They come.'

(10)

On the north side of The Island, sheltered from the ocean storms, was a great inlet to serve as a harbour. High cliffs towered above this inlet and, although the land sloped in one place, much work would have been necessary to make a track from the beach up to the top. There was no place for the Black Pagans to beach their boats, but this did not deter them.

Five boats there were and they rowed right round The Island before putting a horde of warriors ashore on the cliff track. The boats rowed back to the inlet to wait whilst the bearded heathens in their horned helmets swarmed up the track.

The old monk was on his knees in prayer when they dis-covered him and dragged him off to where the Islanders had been herded together. There were no woods to which they might have been able to flee, and little chance for them to hide.

For a little while a few of the Viking leaders laughed as they conferred together, then one of them went to the high cliff looking down on the inlet and waved. One of the boats rowed round to the cliff-track and four men began putting skins of wine ashore.

The old monk had been stripped of his ragged clothes and tied to a post. His tormentors jeeered at his wretchedly thin white and shrivelled body, and Rhiannon blinked back her tears, unable, with her hands tied behind her back to wipe them away. She knew what her own fate would be, yet the serene dignity of the old man somehow gave her courage. He had always told her that the pagans were intent on destroying Jesus and that only by bearing with the most awful things which men could do to them could they ensure that He was not destroyed but would arise again triumphant, just as He rose from the tomb after Calvary.

More drinking horns were filled and passed round and the pagans sang their rough and noisy songs. Then, at last, they lined up to hurl their dreadful axes at their victim. The first two smashed into his ankles, the next into his knees, two more into his shoulders and still, in evident agony and with life slipping away, he contrived to smile at Rhiannon.

Then, his head jerked forward onto his chest. A drunken warrior rushed forward and, swinging his sword aloft decapitated the old man with one violent stroke. Then he impaled the head, dripping blood, on the sword point and ran round his fellows uttering a terrifying war cry.

It seemed to act as a spur to the rest, for now, in their drunken frenzy, they fell upon the women. But they did not fight over Rhiannon. Their leader, a bearded giant, had selected her for himself. With an oath he flung himself upon her and bore her to the ground.

When she would have screamed she somehow conjured up a vision of the old monk's smile in the agony of death and remembered all he had told her of the pagans' determination to destroy the Lord. He must not be destroyed through her.

He would live through her yet. And somehow she endured.

The dry bracken, in ricks and standing, had been fired as dusk was falling, and now, as the flames died down, the pagans, drunk and satiated, also began to grow quiet, heavy with sleep.

In the dim light a small form crawled towards Rhiannon where she lay, barely conscious, in her distress. He had undone the rope which tied her wrists before she was aware of what was happening. As she stirred, her young brother placed his finger to her lips. Somehow, in her agony, she was able to summon up the strength to crawl behind him as he led her, crawling away stealthily, a foot or two at a time.

They were out of reach of further harm before the girl was missed. She heard the drunken bellowing but by that time she and her brother had almost reached the great cave. The tide was out.

Groping their way cautiously in the blackness which enfolded them, they heard seals rushing past them, to be followed by a silence broken only by the lapping of the waves, and found their way at last to the ledge where they settled down to wait.

There was a spring of fresh water which trickled from the rock face, but they had no food. For four nights and three days they hid there until at noon on the fourth day, the boy came back from one of his cautious sorties, peeping round rocks and over cliff-tops, to tell his sister that the boats had gone.

The scene of destruction and brutality brought back waves of remembrance to Rhiannon of the shame and agony she had endured. The women had been raped to death and their bodies, like those of the men, had been mutilated. There was no sign of any children who would almost certainly have been taken off to slavery.

Sheep and cattle had been wantonly slaughtered and only parts of the carcasses cooked for food. There was never much timber on The Island, but everything which could be burned had been reduced to ashes, some of which still smouldered. Rhiannon knelt and prayed.

When she rose, her brother saw tears in her eyes, but there was a look of serenity upon her face.

(12)

It had been a long, hard task for them to dig a hole large enough to take all the bodies of the dead and, when it had been completed, the result was half communal grave and half burial mound. But it served to protect what remained of them from the gulls, crows and buzzards which stripped the carcasses of the slaughtered animals to the bone.

The Black Pagans had taken all the seal skins but they had overlooked a small quantity of barley meal and one whole storehouse full of dried puffins. There were still a few cows and goats in milk, too, so that survival through the winter was possible.

By the springtime, however, Rhiannon was showing heavy with child, so that she and her brother finally decided to repair an old skin craft which had been left unsmashed by the pagans and wait for the first fine day to cross to the mainland.

It was on the mainland that Rhiannon gave birth to her son, and it was there that she made some sort of home with her young brother.

Chapter 2

The Normans

(1)

Jenkyn Wiriott was scarcely more than a toddler as he stood in silence amidst the people round the village green to which they had been summoned by the steward.

John Methelan was a hard man. He liked to think of himself as being fair and just, but, as steward to the Baron, he had his job to do. What should it profit him to treat the man with leniency and thereby call down the wrath of the Baron upon himself if he should come to hear of such leniency? And John Methelan knew that he would have enough enemies to ensure that word would assuredly be sent to his Lordship if there were to be any show of weakness. The case was clear. The man had been taken with a coney in his possession and, worse still, she had young rabbits inside her.

There could be only one penalty, and that was death. And if the people were called to witness the infliction of such penalty it would be more likely to remain with them as a reminder of the value to his Lordship of every coney that might cross their paths for a long time to come.

So the Baron's soldiers had come and tortured the man most cruelly, and then they had hanged him from a gibbet on the village green, and Jenkyn Wiriott had been forced to watch. He did not forget the lesson, especially as he heard older people refer to the fact that the dead coney had been with young. That had been important.

(2)

With his grandmother Jenkyn Wiriott lived. Wise she was, and knew all about the old people and the stories of long ago, but where she was dark complexioned, with brown eyes almost black, Jenkyn was blue-eyed and fair, with strong limbs and broad shoulders, like his father before him.

Jenkyn's mother had died when he was born and his father, in that same year, had been killed whilst going down the cliffs of The Island for sea-birds' eggs. Ever since then he had lived with his Gran, and she made a little money by filling pillows and mattresses with puffins' feathers and selling them.

It was of a winter's evening when her work was done, as they sat by the ball fire, that she first showed him a beautiful bronze bracelet and told him something of its story.

'Long ago,' she said, 'it belonged to a beautiful maid as was ravaged by the Vikings. Terrible cruel times they was.'

'How long ago was it, Gran?'

'I don't know, hon', but when I was a slip of a maid my great grandmother was still alive and she lived to be nearly a hunderd, and she knowed all about it. She it was as towld me and she alus reckoned as it happened about three hunderd years afore that, if not more.'

'Didst thee ever hear tell who the maid was?'

'Oh aye! She was a maid named Rhiannon.'

'Rhiannon.'

'Aye indeed. And that's the name as come down over the years to thy father's mother as thou never didst see.'

'And who was that first Rhiannon then Gran?'

'Oh, she wasn't the first one, hon'. Rhiannon is a mortal owld name. Way back it was Rigantona, then it became Riganton and then Rhiannon. And the Rhiannon of owld was famous in all the stories afore ever these owld Normans or Vikings or Saxons afore 'em ever come about the place.'

Then she told him something of the great legend handed down through the ages about Rhiannon of the old Celtic stories.

There was, she said, a king by the name of Pwyll whose city was known as Arberth. He was Prince of the seven cantrevs of Dyfed and arranged for a royal hunt to be held in the Precelly mountains. Eventually he became separated from the rest of the field and met Arawn, King of Annwn, or hell. They entered into a compact to change places for a year and, in the guise of the King of the Underworld, Pwyll would meet with the beautiful Rhiannon. The idea was that in this way the King of the Underworld could mate with the human Rhiannon to produce a wonder child.

There were many adventures and wonderful happenings before this came about but, eventually, a boy was born in the palace of Arberth. Six women were in attendance, but that night they slept, as did Rhiannon, and when they woke at cockcrow the boy had gone.

Fearful lest they should be accused, the women conspired together. A staghound was in the room with a newborn litter. Killing some of the pups, they smeared the blood on the face of the sleeping queen and strewed the bones on the bed. When Rhiannon awoke they accused her of having slain and eaten her own child.

The chieftains demanded that Pwyll should put Rhiannon away and take another wife. Pwyll, however, refused, saying, 'I promised if my wife proved barren I would put her away, but she has born a son. If she has done amiss let her do penance for her crime.'

Then Rhiannon took counsel of wise men and teachers and, rather than wrangle with the evil women and their lies, she preferred to do penance. The penance was to remain in the court at Arberth for seven years, seated every day by a horse-block outside the gate, and to relate her story to every passer-by who may not have heard it. Then she had to offer to carry her listener to the court on her back.

About this time, the Lord of Gwent Iscoed in Monmouth, one Teyrnon Twryf Liant, known as the best man in the world, had a mare that was the best of mares. Throughout his kingdom neither horse nor mare was more handsome. Each year, on the first of May, she foaled, but never did anyone see the colt. Determined to solve the mystery, the next time the mare was due to foal, Teyrnon took his sword and waited in the stable. Eventually a handsome foal was born and, sure enough, Teyrnon heard a great commotion, and then a huge claw, like that of an eagle, came through the window and seized the colt by the mane. Drawing his sword, Teyrnon hacked off the claw and then, hearing a scream, dashed out into the night. He could find nothing but, on returning to the stable, discovered an infant boy in swaddling-clothes, with a sheet of brocaded silk wrapped around him. When he picked up the boy he found he was very big and strong for his age.

Teyrnon and his wife recognised that the boy was of noble birth, so they had him baptised according to the form of service at that time, naming him Gwri Golden-hair, because his hair was golden, and they reared him as their own. For four years they reared him, and he developed and grew strong far beyond his years, and he rode the beautiful colt.

Eventually Teyrnon and his wife had news of that which had befallen Rhiannon and of the penance which she was having to do. Then Teyrnon gave much thought to the matter, for he had once served under Pwyll, Head of Annwn, and recognised the remarkable likeness of the boy to Pwyll. So Teyrnon and his wife determined to right a great wrong and journeyed to Arberth with the boy.

When they arrived at the court of Pwyll, Rhiannon offered to carry them, but they declined and, when they had told their story, the boy was recognised as the son of Pwyll and Rhiannon, and Rhiannon said, 'Between me and God, I should be delivered of my care if that were true.' So the boy was named Pryderi, meaning care, which was the word his mother spoke when she received the wonderful news of him.

In due course, when Pwyll died, Pryderi reigned in his stead. He added greatly to his kingdom but, being of a wandering nature, arranged a marriage between his mother, Rhiannon, and his friend, Manawyddan, and then arranged for Manawyddan to take charge of his kingdom.

Long into the night Jenkyn listened to his Gran as she told the story, and then, the next evening, she took up the tale again and told of the many further adventures and of Rhiannon's magic birds and many other things.

'Then,' his Gran said, 'they came to the far island out there. Gwales our people call it, but they reckon as the Vikings always knowed it as Grasum. Any road the story was that Rhiannon and her people was there for about four score years.'

'Well how do it come about then Gran,' Jenkyn said, 'as we've got the bracelet now?'

'I don't know exactly hon'. All I really knows is that it have always been handed down. Long after th'owld Romans had gone the Welsh was fighting amongst theirselves and with what was left of the Saxons, and in between times they was marrying each other. Then a couple of hunderd years ago th'owld Normans come and took over, and so it have been gwain on all the time. And in the end the bracelet come down to thy Gramfer. Thee'rt the spit out of his mouth. In looks and ways. He loved that owld Island same as thou doest.'

(3)

As a small boy Jenkyn had been employed in tending the herds and flocks, but his great interest had always been in helping to hunt the conies.

Many years ago, it was said, some of the Barons had brought the first conies over from France. They were still highly prized as a delicacy for the table, a pair of conies being worth more than a dozen hens or fifty dozen eggs.

In some places conygers had been built. Great banks they were, in which the conies could breed. Yet, although they could feed at will upon the Baron's rolling acres, such was the demand for them that they increased but slowly. They had many natural enemies, too, and great were the numbers taken every year by the foxes, stoats and weasels, buzzards and owls.

Jenkyn started young at the herding, for he was big and strong, and his Gran needed the money. Sometimes it was hard, especially in winter when the cold wind and the rain drove over the open land from the cliffs. It was hard in the frost and snow as well, and in the fierce heat of summer it could also be trying sometimes. But there were other days of warm sunshine, when the gentle zephyrs rippled the blue of the sea where the sunlight danced as a myriad sparkling diamonds.

The ways of the wild creatures were as an open book to him and, unlike most of the other children who were engaged in the herding, he was able to read, because his Gran had taught him.

Then came that early summer when, for the first time, he went in the boats with the older men and the boys to The Island, to collect the eggs of the sea-birds, and to take the puffins as they emerged from their nesting places. Pure magic it was as the boats went in under the cliffs where countless thousands of birds called and jostled for position on the ledges. In the air they went in such numbers that they darkened the sun. Upon the water, they seemed to be as many as the stars in the sky in multitude, and as the sand which is by the sea shore innumerable, such as it had been written in the tracts which his Gran had taught him to read.

A dangerous job it could be sometimes for those who went down the cliffs on ropes to collect the green and blue speckled eggs from the ledges, and he never forgot that it was in this fashion that his father had been killed. Even so, The Island seemed to be in his blood for, like his grandfather before him, he loved it.

The grazing on The Island was good. The squire rented it now, and a snug, thatched house had been built where Philpin Le Herde lived with his wife and small daughter, Nesta. All through the year Philpin watched over the sheep and cattle where they roamed freely amidst the ruins of a tribe who had lived there long ago in the days when Rhiannon was there and had been given the bracelet by the young chief who had taken her as his wife. The Island stock were noted for the way they thrived and grew fat beyond anything on the mainland.

(4)

It was upon a day in summer that John Methelan, mounted on a spirited cob, spoke to him upon the road and Jenkyn became sufficiently emboldened to speak his own thoughts.

'Is thy granny keepin' well home there with thee?' enquired the steward, more kindly than might have been expected from one who was known to be so very strict in the matter of his master's interests, especially in regard to the conies.

'Indeed, sir, she be middlin'. And 'tis kind of thee to enquire, sir.'

'A fine 'ooman thy granny and a good long head on her.'

'Indeed, sir. She have learnt me to read very able.'

'Read, thou sayest! And what doest thou read, my boy?'

'The tract, sir. Gran had it gave her years ago by a friar she nursed afore he died.'

'A good 'ooman thy granny. A good 'ooman indeed. And what didst thee read thyself?'

'Twas about Moses, sir, as was leadin' the Israelites out of bondage in Egypt and he laid down laws to help 'em survive. And one of his laws said ''Thou shalt let the dam go that it may be well with thee, and take the young to thee''.'

The steward looked at him keenly. 'Go thee on,' he said, 'Speak what's in thy mind.'

'Well, sir, when I was over after the eggs of the eligugs and the blackbirds on The Island I could see there was no foxes nor stoats and weasels there. And there be only a few buzzards. And I reckons sir, if thou wast to put a few does there with a buck and not let nobody take the does when they be ferretin' but let the does go, then they'd have a far better chance than over here where every mortal thing be after 'em.'

The steward stroked his chin between finger and thumb, then, smiling, drew a purse from his buckskin doublet, threw the boy a silver penny and cantered away.

The steward sent three does and a buck over to The Island and the result had already been spectacular. Within three years there were conies everywhere, and Philpin had begun to complain to the squire of the damage they were doing to the pasture. In springtime they took heavy toll of the young grass, and all through the summer they kept it bare. But, although Philpin's complaints became ever more bitter, John Methelan was delighted, for he knew the returns would be good indeed.

(5)

When the time came that a start was to be made at catching the conies it was but natural that John Methelan should give Jenkyn the chance to go as the second ferreter. He was seventeen at the time.

As he had grown from boyhood to youth and, now, from youth to young manhood, The Island had never ceased to cast a spell on him. Just to go into The Island was enough, with the cliffs towering above the boat as it approached. It was magic, as the birds everywhere dived and swam and flew in wide sweeps and made mighty uproar. The thrift and sea pink flowed over the cliff-tops in great, pink and white swathes, and the scent of bluebells on balmy eve and dewy morn lay heavy on the air.

But that was in the spring-time when he went for the sea-birds' eggs and the puffins. Now it was winter. Yet great was the thrill and exaltation as he roamed the wild cliff-tops where the wind blew fresh and clear, and the salt spray whipped against his face, and the great waves lashed themselves on the rocks far below. Never had he had such sport with the conies on the mainland as they had with them upon The Island that first winter.

They had fashioned nets to place over the rabbit holes, and the red-eyed ferrets, small noses twitching, slid silently into the dark places about their business, and the frightened conies bolted into the nets. Sometimes there would be a hole which had not been noticed, or a net might not have been securely fixed, and a coney would run clear, and then Nimrod, Jenkyn's long-legged dog, would give chase, head near to the ground, and his fierce jaws would make short work of the task he loved.

It was not always that things went so smoothly. Some days, especially if the wind was from the east and blowing cold, the conies were not always so ready to bolt, and then, as likely as not, the men would lose the ferret and have to spend time digging down to see where the ferret would have cornered some coney. They would usually have at least one coney for

their trouble, and sometimes more, but it was small return
for the time and work involved in all the digging.

The day's work done, the ferreters then had to paunch the
conies and skin them. The carcasses were salted down and
the skins were dried to await the steward's men who would
come in the boat to fetch them when the ferreters had
finished.

Although conditions were rough, with Jenkyn and the
ferreter sleeping on bracken in the stable, there were
advantages to living on The Island. Philpin's wife kept hens,
so there were eggs, and they killed a pig every year, and there
was milk from the goats, and there was cheese. Good vegetables, too, they had always grown in the garden, except that
now the conies were finding their way there. So it seemed to
be only justice that many a coney went into the pot. An
allowance of conies had to be made for feeding the ferrets
and the dogs, so nobody would be any the wiser, and good
eating they made, too.

Nor was it only the garden and the pasture where the
conies did damage. There had always been good corn on The
Island, so that there was no shortage of meal, but now the
conies were nibbling away at the young green shoots as they
came through the ground. To that extent Philpin was glad to
see the ferreters coming to catch the conies and reduce their
numbers.

(6)

Jenkyn was pleased that John Methelan, the steward, had
been so receptive to his ideas, and had given him the
opportunity to come here as the ferreter's apprentice, but
there was one aspect that troubled him.

All through the weeks they had been on The Island
catching the conies he had noticed that, when they were
being bolted by the ferrets, it was invariably the does that
were the first to bolt. Perhaps they would be more timid than
the bucks, so this would be understandable.

Then he noticed something else. Whenever they had to dig

to recover the ferret it was always a buck that it had in the corner. So maybe the buck, being bolder, had stood to fight.

For a long time he pondered on this, and he reasoned that, of those conies which had not been caught, there would be many more bucks than does. Yet he had quoted to the steward that Moses had said, 'Thou shalt let the dam go that it may be well with thee.' If he were right in his thinking there might not be nearly so many coneys next winter. But time alone would tell and he kept his own counsel.

In the spring he went again with the men to collect the eggs of the sea-birds and to take some of the puffins. But he also observed, and what he saw disturbed him, for he knew there would not be so many conies in the autumn.

That first winter they had caught nearly two thousand conies, and the steward had waxed expansive in his enthusiasm. In the second winter they had caught scarce a thousand, and John Methelan was ill-pleased. It was then he spoke to Jenkyn, and Jenkyn told him of his thoughts. It was, however, too late to do anything for another year, and in that third winter the catch was no more than five hundred.

There was, however, a difference. They had been careful to let many of the does go. And the following winter they had again caught nearly two thousand. So a policy was laid down accordingly and, now, every winter, they were catching anything up to four thousand conies.

(7)

Jenkyn was a young man of more than twenty summers when his Gran died, and John Methelan, well pleased with his progress, had allowed him to remain in the cottage.

Now, in the winter, he was going into The Island again, this time as the ferreter with a lad to work under him. In the sternsheets they sat, their nets safely stowed, ferrets and dogs seeming to sense the excitement as the men rowed and the rough brown sail carried the sluggish boat away from the shore. But, this year, he was more excited than he had ever been before, and it was an excitement that made him feel his heart hammer so loud that he feared everybody must hear.

The previous year he had talked to Nesta, the herdsman's daughter, and eaten alongside her at table, with a new awareness. No word had he spoken of his feelings, but, during the last weeks before he had returned to the mainland, he had suddenly realised with a quickening pulse that the young girl he had first known had grown to womanhood.

All through the summer he had thought of her but, for more than a week he had been on The Island before a chance came to speak with her alone. Barefooted she went, wild and carefree like a gipsy, black curls blowing, with eyes dark as midnight and skin burnt by summer sun and winter wind. But there was an aloofness about her that Jenkyn could not fathom, although she would colour and drop her glance when, unawares, he looked up to find her looking at him.

It was of a morning, scarce after daybreak, that she came running and called, 'Father the boat is comin'!'

'What be the matter then? It be too soon to come for conies yet.'

'Thou'st better go and see.'

When he came back, agitated and out of breath, he said, 'The master have sent for me.' To his wife he said, 'Thou'st better come with me.'

Nothing loth was she, although she eyed the girl with some misgiving.

'Tis all right, 'ooman. The word is the boat'll bring us back afore nightfall.'

That day, however, which had dawned in autumn splendour full of promise, clouds darkened the sun after Philpin Le Herde and his wife had gone in the boat, and the wind blew contrary. By nightfall Jenkyn knew there could be no boat before the morrow.

At suppertime, when the platters had been cleared and the fire glowed warm, the lad's eyes closed and his head began to droop.

'Thou best away to bed,' said Jenkyn. 'Thou hasn't got used to this island air yet.'

And so, at last, he and Nesta were alone.

'Why hast thou been keepin' out of my way?' he said.

Nesta coloured beneath her tan.

'Why no. What ar't thee talkin' about?'

'I haven't spoke to thee on my own since I come into The Island this time.'

'I been busy.'

'Well, thee'rt not busy now.'

Silence there was then between them and all the things he would have said he could not until, at last, reaching hand inside deep pocket, he drew out the bracelet and held it towards her.

Wide eyed, she fingered the patterned workmanship of it.

'Where didst thee get this?' she said.

'It have been in our family for hunderds of years. My Gran gave it to me afore she died and said my childern must have it one day. But I wants thee to have it.'

'How?'

As he took her in his arms she made to struggle wildly, but even so, he felt her yielding, and then return his kisses with a wild passion. By dim light and in silence he climbed with her to the loft where her bed was. Nothing heard they of the wind as it grew stronger, nor heeded they the time for four days and four long nights as the storm raged about them.

(8)

'I shannot be sorry to go,' said Philpin's wife.

'No, I knows. Thou'st never liked it here.'

'Doest thou have to go?' Jenkyn asked.

'There be nothin' else for it. The master have made up his mind. John Methelan have agreed to lower the rent, and next year it be only some beast and sheep grazin' here and no corn. So 'twill be only somebody to bide here through the summer, and the ferreters in the winter.'

'Well, the Lord takes big profits from the conies.'

'Frig the conies. It be a mortal sin. I can mind the time when the piece of corn we growed was high as a man's head. Now the friggin' conies keeps it as bare as a babby's arse.'

'I wonders what'll happen to the house.'

'Nobody'll bother. This house was built when my gramfer come here and you gotta be doin' somethin' all the time. Specially in the winter. And what'll the ferreters care? So frig the conies.'

'When do we go, Father?' Nesta asked.

'Next fall. After the summer grazin' when the ferreters comes.'

Before Jenkyn left in the early spring Nesta told him she was with child.

He said, 'I'll be back to fetch thee by-an'-by. I got a good cottage an' the steward have promised me a new roof this year.'

(9)

Jenkyn went back into The Island in the spring when the men went for the eggs of the sea-birds, but he spent the day with Nesta. Away from the others they wandered, holding hands, until they came to a quiet place, and there Jenkyn lay with her in the warm sun. He told her of progress with the cottage and how good the steward had been, and they talked much of their plans for the future.

Nesta was not wearing the bracelet. It was too beautiful for that, she said, but she kept it safely and treasured it. One day it would be for their child which she was bearing.

In the autumn they would be coming out from The Island, and she would stay with her father and mother until then. Once again Jenkyn promised her that he would fetch her at that time, before the baby should be born, and the cottage would be all ready for her. Such was the isolated and simple life she had led, that great was her excitement when she thought of having a house of her own.

Jenkyn also told her of the new church. The old wooden church of St Samson, the Celtic saint, had been pulled down, he said, and a beautiful new church of stone, with a stone-slated roof was being built. When it was finished it was to be dedicated to St Mary, the Blessed Virgin.

When Nesta was born, her parents had come out with her to the mainland and she had been baptised. It was the only time she had ever been away from The Island. But the priest had been over to The Island more than once to say Mass. So Jenkyn had spoken to the priest and he had said that when Nesta came out from The Island in the autumn they could be married in the beautiful new church.

The time came at last for Jenkyn to fetch her, and it was the worst autumn storm that even the oldest of the fishermen could remember. The day before Jenkyn was due to fetch Nesta it started, and then the winds howled and tore at the trees and all but the stoutest of buildings for nearly six weeks. Sometimes the storm raged with demonic fury, and the white-capped waves rolled mountains high. Then, when it seemed that it must abate at last, the mayhem erupted again, and Jenkyn fretted, and his whole being knew a great torment.

(10)

Philpin Le Herde had seen the boat and he met Jenkyn as he landed. He was a broken and shattered man, and Jenkyn scarcely had need to ask him how they had fared.

He never saw his lovely young Nesta again, but he knelt and shed bitter tears by the mound above the place where her parents had buried her, and he tried, in his simple, unaccustomed way, to pray.

Her baby was in the rough, wooden crib, with the bracelet with him, and she had asked that he be named Pryderi, for Jenkyn had told her of the old legends of Rhiannon, and he had told her of all that had been told to him of the bracelet. And so, when they came back with heavy hearts to the mainland, Jenkyn took the baby to the priest, and the priest baptised the baby and named him Pryderi.

(11)

With a good cottage refurbished it was but natural that Philpin Le Herde and his wife should move in to live with Jenkyn, and Philpin's wife nursed Pryderi.

Pryderi, like his namesake of old time legend, grew in

strength and stature, and he learned great wisdom of country things from his father.

Jenkyn also prospered. He applied himself faithfully to all the duties that were entrusted to him, and he found favour in the sight of the steward who always gave good reports of him. As John Methelan grew older he began to rely more and more on Jenkyn and he respected his judgement. Then John Methelan died, and Jenkyn Wiriott became the Lord's steward.

The old squire had long since lost interest in The Island. Herdsmen went there in the summer, and ferreters in the winter, but the farming was not what it had been before the conies had been put there to swarm all over the place.

Pryderi married and, like his mother's father, Philpin Le Herde, he had a great interest in the cattle and sheep and everything concerning the land. So Jenkyn Wiriott, the Lord's steward, spoke to the squire, and Pryderi Wiriott took over the squire's lease of The Island to live there with his young wife and to be a farmer.

Great, then, was the activity which followed. The house was enlarged, new outhouses were built, a wall was built all round the garden and, perhaps most important of all, a new track was dug out so that a horse and cart could go all the way down to the beach where the boats landed. It was also much easier to get cattle down the new track into the boat.

(12)

It was not only the sea-birds which provided a harvest from the cliffs in their season but, every autumn, the great grey sea-calves came to breed on the pebbly beaches and in the darkness of the caves. All through the year they were to be seen in the water, sometimes swimming, sometimes suspended in the water with their bewhiskered faces turned towards the cliffs and gazing with their sad, saucer eyes. Sometimes in the sunshine they would heave their great, slug-like bodies onto the outlying rocks, and bask for hours on end, until the incoming tide threatened to wash over them, and they would slide back into the blue depths to seek for fish.

The fishermen did not love them, and they were more than willing to take part in the seal hunt every Michaelmas. For it was after the harvest time that the seals had to come to land to drop their white-furred calves and rear them. Ill-equipped they were to defend themselves on land, apart from their fearsome, sharp teeth. But, with great flippers instead of legs, they could not run and were ungainly, although, as they flapped frantically down the beach in an effort to escape to the sea, the flippers would throw back great pebbles in every direction. Avoid the flying pebbles and the bared teeth and there was no real danger, and a sharp blow on the nose from a heavy stick would kill a seal.

The great bulls were more formidable than the cows but, in any case, did not come to land as much as the cows who had to come to suckle their pups.

The flesh of the sea-calves was good to eat, and a tub of it was worth as much as a tub of pig meat. The fat, too, was full of oil, so it was rendered down and was used for the lights of a winter night.

Then, of course, the pelts were worth money, as well as being made into warm, hard-wearing clothes of all descriptions.

There was one aspect, however, which always lurked at the back of Pryderi's mind and troubled him. Often he had heard the mournful call of the seals in the quiet bays and from the dark caves, and he found it easy to believe some of the stories of those who said that they were inhabited by the souls of people who had died. He knew from his father's teaching long ago that it was good sense for the fishermen to kill the seal cows because they were the ones that bred. 'Thou shalt let the dam go that it may be well with thee, and take the young to thee.' Well, they didn't want it to be well with them as far as the seals were concerned because they ate so many fish. Still, it troubled him.

Then there came to The Island one year a man who had travelled much and he spoke of islands beyond Ireland where they had been killing the seals. One of the men came upon a seal cow suckling her pup in a big cave. He was about to kill the cow when she looked up with tears in her great eyes and spoke to him and asked him not to kill her until her young one should have drunk her fill of milk. But the man paid no heed to her pitiful pleading and killed her all the same. But it brought great misfortune to him because a big wave came into the cave and the man did not come out alive. Indeed, said the traveller, ill fortune would always come upon a man who would do such a thing.

So Pryderi remembered what his father had told him many times, long ago before he died, of how Nesta had died whilst he was being born during the great storm. And Pryderi wondered whether his own father had told him everything and whether he had perhaps ever killed a seal cow with a young one suckling her. For Pryderi could not forget the many stories of those who had lived at the time of the first Pryderi, after whom he had been named, and of all the mysteries surrounding them and their connections with Heaven and the Otherworld. Nor could he forget the tragic story of his own birth and the death of the young mother he had never known. The story of the killing of the seal cow who had pleaded in vain moved him deeply. He did not hunt the seals again.

(13)

The loss from the seals was of small consequence because the grazing on the island was rich. In the course of time Pryderi had acquired the right to take the conies himself and now, remembering his father's teaching, he made sure to kill as many does as possible in order to keep their numbers down.

As time went by, too, it became noticeable that the puffins, which came to The Island every summer to breed, found it very convenient to take over the conies' burrows and, with their great, parrot-like beaks, to drive out the conies during the breeding season.

So, once again, the puffins began to increase and to come to The Island to breed in great numbers.

Chapter 3

The Tudors

(1)

'The folks round that way only ever call it The Island,' John
Wogan said. 'And a good many folks call it the "farm of
birds". But Scalmey is the proper name for it. Ever since the
time of the Vikings.'

Success had come to John Wogan, merchant of the town
and county of Harford, in all his business ventures, but his
son, William, was something of a disappointment to him.
True, he had sailed to the Indies and acquitted himself well in
his dealings there, but there was too much of the dreamer in
him. Up river from Harford he would spend hours watching
the wild ducks and the geese, and he often showed more
interest in affairs of the land than in what could be bought
from those who worked the land.

'It matters not to us, Bill, that they sell their wool.'

'But it does, Father. Better for it to be spun here in the
county than for others to get fat on it.'

'We do well enough out of it, my son. And if the folks round
here are too idle to spin, let it be on their own heads.'

Another thing that troubled the merchant was the fact that
the boy was not far away from thirty and showed no signs of
settling down. The possibility of a visit to Scalmey seemed to
appeal to him.

'You make it sound an interesting place, Father,' he said.

'Well Bill, there's good business to be done there. That I
know. Wiriott is the name of the farmer there, and his family
were there for generations before him. He is staunch in the
old Faith, too, the same as I shall ever be.'

'Does that matter, Father?'

John Wogan pressed his fist on the table.

'It matters to some of us, my son. My father was one of the
first to rally to Henry Tudor's banner when he landed here,
and he marched with him to Bosworth. But the poor old man
would turn in his grave could he but see what Henry's son has

done to Holy Church. He destroyed the monastries and des-troyed much of our farming with it. The money's all been squandered and it'll take years to recover from what he's done in debasing the coinage. Eliot is no friend of mine and he's of the King's persuasion. He's bought Wiriott's wool crop from Scalmey this last ten years, but the word is that Wiriott is not too pleased with Eliot turning his coat.'

'And you think Wiriott will deal with us because of that?'

'No. It means he will be willing to change. And he will sell to us because we can always offer a better price than Eliot.'

'You've heard from him?'

'Yes. He expects you next week, and you shall stay there a night or two if needs be.'

(2)

Everywhere there were puffins. In the air and on the water, along the cliff-tops and outside every rabbit hole. Thousands upon countless thousands, they fluttered and scurried and waddled and croaked.

Never had William Wogan seen anything to compare with it. His father had spoken of the 'farm of birds' but, now he was here, the sight was more than he could comprehend.

Old Wiriott was amused at his wonderment and, as he poured him a goblet of mead, he said, 'Hast thou never saw a puffin afore?'

'Out at sea, but never on land.'

'So thou'st never heard a cocklolly?'

'No indeed.'

'Well, hark for 'em tonight. When there be no moon they calls to each other as they comes in from the sea an' thou's ud think as all the devils in hell had been turned loose. We tells folks as don't know as they be ghosties an' all sorts, but it would never do to tell thee that or we'd never do a deal. Drink up an' let's fill thy goblet.'

It was a happy atmosphere as they sat at table in the cool of the summer evening, and Rhiannon, the farmer's daughter, her auburn hair piled on top of her head, her form lithe as any young fawn as she moved about the room, lent an air of enchantment to match all the wonders that had unfolded for young Wogan that day.

'Have you been here long?' he asked.

'I was born here. Started farming on my own after my father died. And it's a good place to farm. The sheep does well with a wonderful clip of wool and the cattle gets very fat. But my boys wouldn't stop here, and now my wife is dead there be only the two of us. 'Tis a pity to think of nobody to take it on after me.'

'My father said he'd always heard 'twas a poor place to farm because of the rabbits.'

'That was years ago when the Lord had 'em for hisself. They be not worth so much now as they was in th'owld days an' we catches 'em ourselves. The Lord's ferreters used to leave a lot of the does go to breed an' the place was swarming with 'em. But we catches 'em all. But mind thee, the Lord improved the house here and made that good road up from the beach. So now 'tis easy to get cattle down into the boat.'

'My father told me something of how they used to farm for the rabbits.'

'Aye, that was my great gramfer, Jenkyn Wiriott, as started that. Had a wonderful name by all account and finished up as the Lord's steward. Come here first as a young ferreter, and my gramfer, Pryderi, was born here. I've heard tell as his mother was only a young maid and was supposed to go out afore the babby come, but it come on to blow and it blowed for six weeks afore the boat could cross. An' when the boat did come my gramfer had been born an' his mother had died. Only a young maid she was.'

'There seemed to be puffins round all the rabbits' holes.'

'Why aye! The holes be full on 'em. They be nobby little chaps altogether. Them an' the cocklollies. They goes in an' drives them rabbits out a fair masterpiece. Takes over complete for the summer whilst they be nestin'. I've heard tell as the sea parrots and the cocklollies had gone down terrible in numbers till the rabbits come. But now they be nestin' in all the holes everywhere.'

'I'd like to hear the cocklollies.'

'Thous'll hear 'em all right.'

'Wait till midnight,' said Rhiannon, 'and it'll be like a mad-house for an hour or two.'

(3)

It was close on midnight as they went out into the freshness of the night air and Rhiannon had put a cloak round her shoulders. Her father had already excused himself and gone to bed.

Everywhere was a silence such as William Wogan had never known. Stars shone far above and he knew a great peace.

'You are very lucky to live in such a place.'

'It's not like this in winter. It can be wild and rough then.'

'Do you mean you don't like living here?'

'I love it. I was born here.'

'And you don't want to leave?'

'When you've lived on an island all your life you learn to live a day at a time and you take things as they come.'

'Did you go to school?'

'No, never.'

'Yet you speak nicely.'

'I learned to read when I was young. I had a nurse who taught me much.'

'You are so beautiful you could be a great lady.'

He saw her even white teeth as she smiled in the darkness and he knew her green eyes would be dancing as she said, 'But I am a great lady.'

'Indeed? I should have known.'

'Oh yes, tomorrow I will show you.'

'You mean you have proof?'

'Proof, yes. In bronze.'

'But you don't need proof. I knew as soon as I saw you on the beach when the boat landed.'

'There! Listen!' and she held up her hand.

Beneath their feet in the darkness, from somewhere under-ground, came a low purring or growling noise. Presently it was joined by another and then, of a sudden, from out of the darkness and from no great distance, came a shriek as of a soul in torment.

'Mother of God and merciful Christ,' he said, crossing himself, 'What was that?'

Rhiannon laughed but, before she could answer, the call had been taken up and was being echoed and repeated all around them.

'The cocklollies or cockels,' she said. 'Thus known because of their call, but known by the scholars as shearwaters. Said by the fishermen to be the souls of drowned seamen in eternal torment roaming the deep.'

Then all about them was noise such as could scarce be described, and dim shapes flapped close to their faces as wild shriek followed wild shriek.

For an hour and more, as though they were part of the unearthly chorus, they strolled on through the grass, now heavy with dew, till the sound began to fade and, as suddenly as it had started, it died away and everywhere was a great silence. A cricket chirped and glowworms scattered their incandescent lights along the way.

'This is magic,' he said at last. 'Pure fairyland. But we've come a long way from the house. Is that the sea I can hear?'

'Yes, just coming up onto the pebbles.'

'Then we have a long walk back.'

'No, there's a short cut. But be careful how you go.'

As he hesitated in the darkness she offered him her hand. He was still holding it when they reached the end of the winding path and she made no attempt to remove it.

At the door of the house he took her other hand as well and bent to kiss them tenderly.

(4)

William's two days visit had lengthened to four days and not through any quirk of wave or wind or weather. For days on end what gentle breeze there was had come from the south as it followed the sun round all day. Thrift and sea campion drenched the cliffs in pink and white, and the merest swell of the ocean did no more than lay white wavelets gently at the foot of the great cliffs. Far below them razorbills and guillemots dived and swam way down in the clear blue depths.

Puffins were everywhere, more numerous than daisies, as he walked on the close-cropped green sward, hand-in-hand with the girl whose glory of auburn hair hung rippling to her waist.

Intoxicated with a headiness which no mead could ever have induced, he knew he had offered far more for the wool clip than he had intended, even though prices were holding firm and his father reckoned that prospects were improving. Content with their own company and the magic that was everywhere about them, they walked on until they came to an eminence from which they gazed far out across the ocean, all round the island and, beyond the treacherous sound, smooth-running now, to the mainland which disappeared in a haze at the tip of the great sweep of the bay.

'Is this not a beautiful kingdom?' Rhiannon said as she sat down with her arms round her legs and her chin on her knees.

'Beautiful indeed. And with a beauty that is matched only by the matchless beauty of the princess who rules over it.'

'You think I'm a princess?'

'Never a doubt of it.'

'When I was a small girl I used to sleep with the bracelet under my pillow sometimes, and then I would come up here and sit and dream beautiful daydreams about a handsome prince coming in a great ship with a beautiful snow-white sail to claim me for his own.'

'And did you sail away over the horizon with your handsome prince?'

'No never. Or if I did, I always came back. I couldn't bear the thought of leaving here.'

'What is the real story about the bracelet, d'you know?'

'Only what I've told you. They say that Jenkyn Wirriot, who became the Lord's steward, gave it to his young wife, Nesta, when he was a young ferreter. The girl who died here in childbirth. And when he arrived, and she was dead, the bracelet was in the crib with the little baby. That was my father's grandfather, Pryderi.'

'It would be nice to know.'

'The only other thing I've ever heard was from a very old woman on the mainland who used to come here sometimes in the summer for cheese-making when we had many more goats. And she used to say that it had something to do with an earlier Rhiannon who was ravaged and had a child by one of the Vikings and that the bracelet had been here as long as the puffins.'

'That cannot be.'

'I suppose not. Because they must have been coming here since time began.'

'But it makes you a princess.'

She looked at him seriously. 'Oh, no,' she said, 'I'm a princess on my mother's side.'

'Your mother?'

'Yes, it's from her I get my hateful red hair.'

'It is beautiful.'

'It is hateful. She was pure Welsh and her great grandmother, I think it was, maybe even further back than that, was a daughter of David, the last Welsh prince.'

'But Llewellyn was the last Welsh prince.'

'Don't believe it. David, his brother, fought on for nearly a year after Llewellyn had been killed and before he was himself so brutally murdered by the English, torn apart by their horses and then beheaded. The same monsters who are trying to force their new religion on us. His daughters were put into a convent in England but one ran away and was never caught. She went with a young Welsh drover they say.'

Taking her hand he said, 'Could one of such proud lineage consider a very humble merchant if he were to ask for her hand in marriage?'

For long, searching moments she looked at him and seemed to be satisfied with what she read in his earnest gaze.

(5)

Old man Wiriott was well-pleased with the turn of events, especially as young Wogan showed such great interest in The Island and in everything that was happening there. John Wogan, too, was not dissatisfied to see his son settle down as he called it. He could still play his part in the merchant's business, and eventually there could be grandsons to follow him.

William Wogan did indeed prosper and became rich, with many ships at his command. Fine seamen were undertaking voyages of great daring and opening up trade routes all over the world. But piracy was rife upon the high seas and island dwellers around the coasts were particularly vulnerable to their depredations. William Wogan mounted a small canon, known as a murtherer, on the cliff above the track commanding a fine sweep of the landing beach, and his farm servants given some rough drill in the use of arms. For whatever reason, his household was not troubled by pirates in the years he was on The Island.

With the increase in trade, farming also prospered, although it was hard for some where sheep were taking over from corn and some were losing their land.

William Wogan's empire, however, remained secure, and might have gone to even greater strength had he not been drowned when crossing to the mainland. No grandson did he leave, Rhiannon having borne him just one daughter.

Rhiannon never recovered from the shock, and her loss was more grievous than she could bear. Eventually her mind became deranged and, for hour after hour, she would wander the cliff-tops gazing out to sea and mumbling incoherencies of her prince coming to claim her.

Then came a night in winter when she did not return. She was never seen again, and Scalmey fell into other hands.

Chapter 4

The Stuarts

(1)

Of the daughter of Rhiannon Wiriott and her husband, William Wogan, nothing is known, neither of where she went nor whom she married. Nor, for close on a hundred years, was anything known of the bracelet.

They were years of religious turmoil and political treachery, suspicion and persecution. Heavy demands were made upon the yeomen, and feuds were bitter. Then came a time when Walsingham's spies were everywhere in the Queen's service, but there came, too, a time of great material prosperity, until the land was plunged again into all the ills of former days.

The seafarers, however, had brought home much wealth and gained great possessions. And it was at this time that once again the bracelet is known to have remained in the family in whose possession it had been since time out of mind.

(2)

'When good Queen Bess was on the throne,' Pryderi Whitton was saying, 'It was different. But it looks as if we'll never see them days again.'

As the schooner, the Alice May, heavily laden, ran before the wind, which was blowing hard now from the south west, her planks groaned and the wind whistled through the stays as they took the strain of the great billowing sails. White caps were already topping the waves, and the troughs between them were already growing steeper.

'Keep her as she goes, Mister.'

His sharp, blue eyes, set wide and fearless in his weather-beaten face, for a long time had been scanning the horizon as he spoke, and then, as the vessel was lifted high in the water, the drizzle was suddenly blown away and he said, 'There she is.'

Even in the poor light Scalmey was seen, rising dark and forbidding above the white foam that boiled beneath its mighty cliffs, and had loomed up within sailing distance.

'Well, nightfall we said. And once we can get into the haven there it can blow as hard as it like. Starboard of the Wolves Teeth, Mister, for we'll have the Dead Man's Race with us from there.'

Riding at anchor in the haven under the lee of the great cliffs they were conscious of nothing more than a heavy swell and the wind troubled them not at all.

A seaman came to clear the platters from the master's trim cabin and put a jug of ale on the table. Left to themselves Whitton said to his companion,

'This is my last trip. I've had enough. I served with Drake when he went out to meet the Armada, and I sailed with Raleigh to the Americas. All my life we was fightin' the Spanishers an' I wouldn' ha' wished a dog to be treated like we was treated by our own officers. I got lash marks on my back as I had when I was a crut too small to lift a pail of water.'

He topped up their goblets from the jug and his companion took a pinch of snuff from the back of his hand.

'Aye,' said Whitton, 'they were mortal hard times. But we felt 'twas worth it because we nearly drove the Spanishers off the seas, the country was gettin' stronger an' trade have never been better. But what we got to show for it now? A bloody Scotch man on the throne hand in glove with the papists again and makin' up to the Spanishers as I spent all my life fightin'.'

His companion, dressed very much in the latest fashion, from powdered wig, right down to the silver buckles on his high-heeled shoes, still said no word and Whitton raised his great bulk out of his chair and yawned. He smiled, 'I've had ten good years an' I'm satisfied. We'll collect my little maid on the way back an' you can do what you like with the ship. I'll leave my share until it's convenient to buy me out, but my sailin' days is over.'

Miles Aundle, heavy-lidded of eye and with voice as

smooth as his appearance, spoke at last. 'You won't change
your mind?'

The master made no answer. They had discussed it all
before.

'This young captain. Can I rely on him?'

'I sailed with his father. He's young, yes. But he's a
Cardiganshire man out of Aberporth and they don't come no
better.'

'And your daughter?'

'What about her?'

'Will she want to come with you?'

'I hopes so. But the folks here on The Island won't stay
much longer anyhow. The raids from the pirates is more than
they can stand an' they're gettin' older, too, the same as me.'

'How old is your daughter?'

'She be comin' up to fifteen now.'

'Could be trouble for you.'

'Not if she take after her mother.'

(3)

Long before mid-morning the sun was shining, and the
stillness beneath the great cliffs seemed far away from the
storm, which had threatened on the previous evening, but
which had now blown itself out.

Everywhere on the ledges there were countless thousands
of sea-birds, eligugs and razorbills, groaning and croaking
and jostling for position. On the water the puffins had
collected for their morning swim and cleansing.

From under a neatly contrived and cunningly fashioned
canopy three sailors had rolled out on deck a demiculverin
and, having charged it with powder, were now, with much
coarse laughter, filling it with a dozen pounds of small nails
and tacks. Pryderi Whitton and his companion, along with
the rest of the crew, watched them ram down the wad and
then sight the murderous weapon along the surface of the
water.

As the roar of the gun boomed and echoed from the cliff-
face, birds churned the water to rise in mad, splashing terror

from its surface, in massed clouds they launched themselves from the ledges from which eggs in their hundreds came cascading and smashing down, and the sun was darkened by the living blanket which soared and whirled in blind confusion.

Upon the water, as blood now mingled with it, several dozen puffins lay lifeless or fluttered helplessly. A small boat was lowered and two of the crew were dispatched to collect the spoils.

'They be wonderful good eatin',' said the master. 'Tastes like fish. That's how the papists eats 'em in lent.'

As they leaned over the rail watching, a boat put out from the quayside with The Island farmer.

Once on board he went below with Whitton to his cabin.

'An' how's my little Rhiannon?'

'She've growed. An' thou'st got to take her off this trip.'

'I'm goin' to. But how art thee so worried lookin'?'

'We've had the pirates again. Last month. I knowed they was headin' for The Island when I sighted their boat, so I left some sheep in the yard an' the dairy door open with the cheeses an' then locked ourselves in the house. But that wasn't enough for 'em. They tried to batter down the door an' I was afraid for the maid.'

'Christ alive man. What happened?'

'I shot one of 'em from the window and th'others took to their heels. But they'll be back.'

'What about the one thou shot?'

'They left'n where he was and I buried'n in the field.'

Whitton poured two goblets of ale.

'Is she agreeable to come with me?'

'Aye, she be afeard. She be owld enough now to understand. She don't want to leave the wife but she be ready to come.'

'Good.'

Going to an iron-banded chest he unlocked it and took out a small leather bag from which he tipped a large handful of doubloons on the table. Matthew Johns looked at the pile of gold coins wide-eyed. Then Whitton scooped them back into the purse, re-tied the tape, and, putting his hand on the other man's shoulder, said,

'I shall never be out of thy debt Matt. But here's some small bit of thanks for what thou'st done.'

'Thou knows there's no need for this Pryderi. But I won't say it won't be useful.'

'How are things goin'?'

'Not so good again now. We had some wonderful good years with the corn, but now the pirates have started again it be a job to keep farm servants here. I haven't put no corn in this year and in the autumn I'll be packin' up. The rent is more than double what it was.'

'Good God! Still double?'

'Why aye. The Squire went over campaignin' against th' Irish that time and had to raise money somehow an' all the rents was rose an' there they've stayed ever since. 'Tis main serious on a lot of us now. An' with the pirates on top of everythin' it be more than a man can manage.'

'Hast thou got any corn to load this time?'

'Aye. There be about eight hunderd bushels left from last year's harvest and that be the lot.'

'Good. 'Twill be enough. I got a fine load of silk, brandy and tobacco. Took it aboard out in the channel. We can unload it tonight, an' tomorrow we'll load the corn an' sail for Cardigan. If there be any of the King's men watchin' the cliffs so much the better. The small boats'll be across after we've gone. Thous'll get the message.'

'Thous'll be comin' up with me now?'

Lowering his voice, Whitton said, 'No. My respects to Liza. But I got a customer aboard I don't trust over much. 'Twould be a terrible thing if he got some notion in his head to take over the ship whilst I was ashore. I got a young man takin' over from me when we reaches Cardigan an' he'll know how to manage things. So bring thee Rhiannon down tomorrow when we loads the corn.'

(4)

It had not been part of Pryderi Whitton's plan to collect Rhiannon so soon on this trip, but he could make arrangements.

His biggest concern was Miles Aundle. The short answer was that Whitton did not trust him and, the more he saw of him, the less he liked him. He had no wife but women a many, and was of an age when he should have been married if those were his intentions. It was by chance, and not of Whitton's volition, that Aundle had joined him in business.

As Clerk to the magistrates he was privy to most of what was happening amongst the Free-traders, of whom Pryderi Whitton was an active member. But, withal that their activities were outside the law, because the law was stupid and vexatious, Pryderi was an honourable man according to his own lights.

Two of the magistrates had shares in the Alice May and were content with anything extra by way of brandy, tobacco or salt that fell to their lot. As Clerk, Aundle was well taken care of and had always been treated more than generously. But Aundle was a greedy man and became more demanding. When his demands were not met, unbeknown to Whitton he bought a number of shares in the vessel. Whitton still had the largest number of shares, and continued as master, but he began to have misgivings. If Aundle were to get together with some of the other share-holders things could become unpleasant.

He had had some good years with 'the trade'. With his friendship with Matt Johns on Scalmey he had great advantages. Let the King's men spy and patrol where they liked they would always be at a disadvantage. There were so many coves and creeks and inlets right along the bay, and all up the Haven, that the sloops and smacks only need bide their time and wait their chance to call at The Island and collect their modest cargoes, a little for one and a little for another, whilst the preventives looked for something bigger.

Pryderi had been well content and had always organised his own cargoes and contacts. Now, however, Aundle had

started to arrange the occasional cargo, and Pryderi Whitton
had found himself dealing for the first and last time with Tom
Salkeld, the notorious pirate who had captured and made his
base on Lundy. It confirmed him in his opinion that it was
time to get out and settle down. Sooner or later he would
have a fight on his hands with which he would be unable to
cope. The time had come to make way for a younger man.
He, too, had his contacts and he, too, could do things
unbeknown to others. No more than himself did the two
magistrates want to become involved with Salkeld and his
murderous confederates, and they sold their shares to
Whitton. He, in turn, made his own arrangements with a
young sea captain, Owen Griffiths, of Aberporth.

Pryderi Whitton had every reason to believe that the Alice
May would be in good hands. His money would be wisely
invested, and profitably too, as long as they steered clear of
the wrong people.

(5)

Rhiannon had not only grown taller since last Pryderi
Whitton had seen her. Her figure was fuller and he could see
she was a child no longer. One glance at her shapeliness was
enough to confirm that Matt's fears on her account were
well-founded. As he picked her up and held her to his chest
her father knew an unspeakable horror at the thought of
what the bestiality in man could do to her, and waves of
awful recollection swept over him and she felt him tremble
violently. When he put her down his weathered cheeks were
wet with tears.

Now, however, their cargo had to be put ashore, fresh
water had to be taken on board, and the corn loaded, and the
schooner was under way and clear of the wind-tumbled
waters of the tide race before he had time to talk to her in
earnest. The wash rolled back from the prow and its invigor-
ating spray salted their faces as they leaned on the rail and
watched the coast slide past them.

'And how doest thee like th'idea of comin' to live with thy
father at last?'

'I'm glad.' Her brown hair hung loose to her shoulders in long flowing waves which lifted in the breeze. She had her father's blue eyes, but her wide forehead and dimpled chin were the features of her mother.

'Really glad?'

'Yes. I'll miss Liza and Matt but I'm afeared now since the last time the pirates came.'

'Aye, men can be brutal and lower than the beast of the field.'

He put his arm round her shoulders and held her gently to him.

''Twill be safe from 'em when we gets ashore.'

'No more puttin' to sea?'

'No. This is the last trip an' I got a nice little house ready for us to go to with a good garden an' enough money to last us to th'end of our days. There'll be no more puttin' to sea.'

She pressed her head against his chest.

'I'm glad of that,' she said, 'I could never abide the thought of what mother must ha' suffered.'

Rhiannon felt him stiffen suddenly and he held her away from him.

'What doest thee know of that my child?'

'Only what Liza told me.'

'When did she tell thee?'

'After the pirates been last time. She was mortal upset an' afeared.'

'An' what did she tell thee?'

'How Mother died an' what they done to her first.'

Then she saw the look of agony on her father's face and took his great caloused hands in her own.

'Was it terrible Father?'

'Ah, my child. Never speak on it. 'Twas th'only time I'd ever took her on board. Thou was't only a bitty mite only a few months owld. Four boys we had. Owlder than thee an' they'd all died of the plague. So we thought th' only hope was for thy mother to come to sea with thee in her arms. But oh dear Jesus, 'twould ha' been better for us all to ha' died of the plague a thousand times.'

'Was it the pirates?'

'No, my child. 'Twas the Spanishers. Worse than any pirates they be with their fiendish cruelty. Tied to the mast I was an' forced to watch. When they'd done with her sweet body 'twas a blessin' from the good Lord to see her die.'

Rhiannon lifted his hands to her lips.

'Tell me all now, Father. Then we'll never speak on it again.'

'There's little more to tell, my child. Because of thee their captain spared me. They put us both in an open boat with some food, an' chucked in a couple of blankets an' a trunk, then turned us adrift. The next day we was picked up by a vessel sailin' north an' the cap'n agreed to put us ashore on The Island. I'd knowed Matt an' Liza for years. An they've looked after thee for me ever since.'

He looked longingly then towards the land and said, 'But that's all gone an' done now an' we got the future to look to. So come thee down below to my cab'n an' I'll give thee somethin' as I been savin' for when thou hast growed up.'

It was a bracelet of richly burnished bronze that he gave her, toothed and of delicate workmanship. It was penannular and finely sprung.

The girl fingered it admiringly.

''Tis beautiful,' she said. 'Is it to be mine?'

'Aye indeed. When thou wast born thy mother said 'twas for thee.'

'Where did it come from?'

'I don't rightly know. But years ago it belonged to one of thy mother's people who lived on The Island. The 'ooman's husband was a very rich merchant as was drowned crossin' to the mainland. An' the story goes that this poor soul, who was by all account a lovely lookin' 'ooman with red hair, went off her head an' got the' idea as she was a princess. I've heard tell as she wandered The Island lookin' for her prince all out about the cliffs an' then one night she went out an' never come back. I was related somehow as well, which was how I was named Pryderi, but I don't know how.'

Rhiannon put the bracelet on her arm and held it away so that she could admire it that much the better.

'I'll wear it for today,' she said. 'Then I'll put it away an' keep it for my grandchildren when I'm old like Liza.'

(6)

Pryderi Whitton had much to occupy his mind for the rest of the voyage, but he was shrewd enough to notice the little compliments which Miles Aundle paid Rhiannon, and how he charmed her with his studied courtesies and his easy talk of what the ladies wore, and how they conducted themselves in the circles of fashion. Nothing loth was Pryderi, when they berthed at Cardigan, to welcome Owen Griffiths on board as the new master of the Alice May.

Not over tall, the young seaman was broad shouldered, with black, curly hair and shrewd brown eyes that missed nothing, and yet could wrinkle in a smile of homely warmth. His clean-shaven chin was strong and his jaw firm. Pryderi had no doubts about the wisdom of his choice.

For almost an hour the two men were deep in talk in the master's cabin, and then Whitton surprised Miles Aundle by announcing that he and Rhiannon were leaving the ship. From Cardigan they went by one of the small coastal smacks to be put ashore at Aberporth, and from there it was scarce an hour's walk to the house that was waiting for them.

Much newer than the old house on Scalmey it was, and Rhiannon loved everything about it, from her own cosy bedroom overlooking the distant bay, to the stone-flagged dairy, with its pots and great pans scrubbed and shining. Oak the timber was, right through, and driven into the great beams in the kitchen were hooks to hang the hams and sides of bacon.

There was a lovely garden, too, with an orchard where there were bee-hives, and there was more than enough land, her father said, to keep a cow for the house. Hens there would be, as well, and ducks and some geese if she wanted them. And Meg was there to greet them. Megan Pugh, who lived down the lane, and whose husband kept some sheep in the summer and fished for herrings in the autumn. But he had no boat of his own, and already Pryderi had agreed to buy a smack so that they could work it together.

A great delight Meg had taken in making sure that everything was clean and shining, and the fire burning, to greet them when they arrived. She spoke English, too, which was a help for Rhiannon, who was not familiar with the Welsh, and that was the language nearly everybody else spoke, for they knew no English at all. But Megan had come from the south country and had only picked up the Welsh since she married Ianto.

So, when Pryderi Whitton died, Rhiannon had to rely very much on Meg, because she had learned but little Welsh. And she was still scarcely eighteen years of age.

Owen Griffiths was at sea in the Alice May when it happened, and Rhiannon would have been glad to have had him to turn to. Worse still, she had no idea how long it would be before the Alice May would be sailing back into Cardigan.

Not much to say was there with Owen, yet an air of confidence he always had about him, and Rhiannon knew how much her father had respected his judgement, and how he had approved of the way he ran his ship. Pryderi Whitton still held the controlling share, and he always said it was a safe investment and that their money was in good hands. But it was nigh on a twelvemonth since she had last seen Owen, and so it was that, longing as she was for the chance to talk to him, she was more thankful than she could have explained to be able to turn to Miles Aundle instead when he came to offer his sympathy and his help.

Very smooth was Aundle in his talk at the Ship Inn at Tresaith, where he had taken a room, and where he impressed them with his scholarship for, not only did he speak their language, but he wrote poetry in Welsh as well, so it was said.

In the springtime it was, and that was a time of year when Rhiannon always knew she would find herself thinking of Scalmey and the happy days of childhood. Now, once again, as the sun danced on the diamonds out in the bay, she thought with longing of the puffins, white upon the cliff-tops like so many daisies, and she could almost smell the fragrance of the bluebells and needs must close her eyes to keep back the tears.

It was easy for the courteous, smooth-talking Miles Aundle to persuade her that they must travel to Bristol to see into the business of the Alice May. She was not to know that the few shares he still held were of small moment. And when he spoke of new clothes, and the fashions of the day, she was almost eager to go. Any suspicions were put away from her.

Meg was not so easily convinced, however, for, out in the boat together, more than once had Pryderi told Ianto what he thought about Miles Aundle. Fortunate indeed was it for Rhiannon that, the day after she sailed with Aundle, word came that the Alice May had docked at Cardigan. So Ianto took the Welsh cob and rode him till he was in a lather of sweat. Fortunate was it, too, for Rhiannon that they knew the sloop on which they had sailed, and that Owen Griffiths knew she was bound for Bristol. On the next tide but one, the Alice May, in balast, was also bound for Bristol and crowding on full sail.

Berthing at the Welsh Back at Bristol, Owen noted a number of ships he knew, and his keen eyes soon spotted the sloop he sought. Within the hour he found her master carousing at a dock-side tavern. He was not too far gone in drink to understand the earnestness of Owen's request for information.

'All I want to know,' said Owen, 'is where Aundle took the girl.'

'What's it to you?' the man said. Shifty eyed, he seemed to Owen to be the sort of man with whom Aundle would deal.

'Never mind what it means to me. But I'll tell you what it means to you. It means two guineas if you tell me by the time I count ten.'

'And if I don't?' The man had taken sufficient drink to be truculent.

'If you don't tell me,' Owen said very quietly, 'I'll drag you outside and beat the shit out of you. And then you'll tell me. It might take ten minutes longer, but you'll tell me. It's only to save time that I'm offering you the two guineas instead. And if anything has happened to the girl I'll come back and beat the shit out of you anyway. Now then, I'm counting . . .'

Within ten minutes Owen had found the lodging house he sought. A middle-aged woman, of none too tidy appearance, shuffled to answer his loud knock on the front door, which she opened but a few inches, yet far enough for Owen to put his foot in to prevent it being shut.

'What d'you want?' she said.

'I don't want trouble,' said Owen. 'I'm looking for somebody.'

'Who you looking for?'

'A young lady.'

'There's no young lady here.'

'I've a guinea in my pocket that says there is.'

The woman seemed to be weighing him up.

'Show me,' she said.

In one quick movement she pocketed the guinea and opened the door.

'In there,' she said, nodding to the sitting room, and left him.

Rhiannon had already realised Aundle's designs, not only on herself, but on her controlling share in the Alice May. Before she knew it she was in Owen's arms and sobbing out her story whilst he stroked her brown hair.

'First of all,' he said, 'we must get you back to the Alice May.'

'And then? What then?'

'Then I'll go look for Aundle. What was the paper you signed?'

'I don't know. I just made my mark and the man with him said that would be all right.'

'Don't you worry about that. As long as you're all right. That's all that matters for the moment.'

'Will you get the paper back?'

'I shouldn't wonder,' he said, and kissed her on the cheek.

She clung to him again then. She had always known that her father had chosen wisely.

(7)

In the dim light of the tavern Owen Griffiths stood for several minutes, back to the wall and watching carefully.

In his ruffles and lace Aundle seemed somewhat out of place. His two companions were less ostentatiously dressed, but they all seemed well pleased with themselves. Aundle called for a fresh flask of wine and refilled their goblets. There was an inkhorn and writing pens on the table.

Raising his goblet Aundle said, 'Let us drink to the new master of the Alice May.'

'Not just yet,' Owen Griffiths said quietly from behind him.

Aundle pushed back his chair and came to his feet as he spun round.

'There's a saying in your county,' Owen smiled, 'Brighter birds have sung at the top of the tree in the morning but the cat have had 'em afore night.'

'What d'you want here?' Aundle slurred.

'I want the document that you tricked Miss Whitton into signing earlier today.'

Aundle saw the menace in Owen Griffiths' eyes and fumbled to draw a pistol from his pocket. Before ever he could remove it Owen had Aundle's wrist in a grip of iron and his arm behind his back. In the seaman's other hand, as if by magic, there had appeared a murderous looking knife, the point of which was at Aundle's throat.

'The paper,' Owen said.

'I tell you . . .' but the knife pricked Aundle's throat.

'It's in my pocket.'

Owen nodded to one of Aundle's companions. 'Take the paper out,' he said.

The knife pricked Aundle's throat again and he almost sobbed, 'Do as he says.'

An ominous silence had fallen on the smoke filled room. A woman laughed shrilly over in a far corner. Owen wondered whether he had been wise, in his fury, to come here alone. Then from behind, he heard a voice say, 'Popeth yn iawn, Griffiths,' and he smiled grimly to himself. So there was at least one Welshman there, and probably a Cardi. He would not be completely outnumbered.

The paper safely transferred, Owen Griffiths said, 'Now then, Aundle, I name you liar, thief and rogue. And for honest men to know you in future I'll leave a mark on you.' And, almost quicker than eye could see, the knife had sliced across Aundle's forehead and the blood was trickling down into his eyes. Then, as the hubbub broke out, Owen Griffiths slipped out into the gathering darkness, and the Alice May sailed with the tide.

That same year Rhiannon and Owen were married, and it was the start of a long, happy and financially successful marriage.

In the first years of their married life Rhiannon made a couple of voyages with her husband to foreign parts and, having been brought up on Scalmey, always felt at home on the sea. Then, when their first child was due, they bought a farm. Already they had bought out all the shares in the Alice May, and then they bought another ship.

(7)

As their business grew, Owen Griffiths gave up the sea. Whenever a new boat was built at Cardigan or New Quay he and his wife would try to buy shares in it and, gradually, they also added to their own fleet. Owen had recognised the importance of the coastal trade, and soon he became a merchant as well, supplying the needs of the farms and householders over a wide area.

Then as their family grew, and their business expanded and flourished still further, they built a mansion, with a home farm, in the lovely Vale of Teify, where the black cattle grew fat and the salmon were beyond compare. Mahogany for the panelling came from foreign parts in one of their own ships, and their own vessels brought rare and exotic plants to adorn the grounds.

The Griffiths were strong in their religion, too. Rhiannon remembered how her father had inveighed against the papists, who went to mass of a Sunday and then, for the rest of the day, were doing all manner of things, and taking part in all manner of sports, unbecoming to the Sabbath. Equally, Owen Griffiths' family and their countrymen, fervent Welshmen all, had never been enthusiastic for the Reformed Faith, which the English had tried to impose on them, and Owen was strong among the Dissenters.

By the time he died, fifty odd years after he and Rhiannon had married, they were people of property, wealth and some influence.

Chapter 5

The Hanoverians

(1)

White of hair, the old lady walked slowly with the aid of a stick, but her skin was still clear and her blue eyes were bright and alert. Rhiannon Griffiths' broad forehead was even yet a marked feature of her once handsome face.

Her great-grandson, her first, although she had many grandchildren, adored her and was forever asking her to tell of The Island and her life there as a girl.

''Twas hard in many ways,' she said. 'But, oh, 'twas wonderful in the springtime when the birds came. And all through the summer they'd be about the cliffs and 'twas lovely to walk there when the wind was blowing and to roam the cliff-tops wild and free. Then once a year the men would go down the cliffs on ropes for the sea-birds' eggs and some of the sea-parrots would be took for their down. Wonderful good stuff it was for the pillows and the mattresses.'

There were stories, too, of great sailing ships, slave trading, smugglers, pirates and desperate encounters at sea. These stories, however, appealed to him but little. It was of The Island he wanted to be told and of the sheep and horses that were bred there.

Pryderi knew that his father owned ships, but he also owned the big house where the boy lived with the old lady, and it was here that he came to know and love the calves and cows, the sheep and the great horses. Especially did he love the sturdy Welsh cobs and, from a very early age, he had his own sure-footed mountain pony, and all day he would be about the farm with the men and the farm boys, up with the pony amongst the heather and the wild mountain sheep, where the grouse flew strong, and the curlew's liquid call haunted the lonely moors.

It was on a day when he had come from the fields that his great-grandmother sent for him. That day she had not stirred from her room and she lay with her frail hand on the counterpane. In it she clasped a bronze bracelet.

(2)

Pryderi's mother had died when he was born and, for a time after old great grandma Rhiannon died, he was left to his own devices. About the fields and the moors all day in all weathers he grew strong and tall. Then his father said the time had come to apply himself to study. He had had tuition of a sort, but his father reckoned that, with the commercial empire which would one day be his, something more was necessary.

Iestyn Griffiths was a cheerful man and business was his life. Pryderi had no wish to oppose him but, try as he would, he could evince little interest in the sea-trade which had been the basis of their fortune. He knew that his future lay with the land. Once, great grandma Rhiannon had told him of a girl on The Island who was one of those who had owned the bracelet and from whom he was descended. Nesta her name was and her father had been the herdsman. It was in his blood.

Even so, he was not averse to study. He enjoyed reading and believed there was much to learn about the land and the animals, and he believed that knowledge could be applied to produce more and to obtain better results.

But, of course, when it came to talking of university, there was the harsh reality that Oxford lay many miles distant over rough tracks and wild mountain passes. Isolated, with the sea as their main, if not quite their only, means of transport, they lived in a world of their own. Dublin, however, across the Irish Sea, was much more easily accessible with a regular service available.

It was at University in Dublin that Pryderi met his fellow countryman, Rupert de Clare. Haughty at first, in the knowledge that his family had come over with the Conqueror, Pryderi was not slow to tell him that his own people had been there much longer and had never been conquered anyway.

Pryderi, if he was anything at all, was, like his family, a Dissenter. But Rupert was staunch Catholic, and had much in common with some of the young Irish people he met in their hatred of Cromwell and the devastation he had wrought upon their land. In this they had Pryderi's sympathy, too, and he and Rupert became good friends by the time Pryderi was due to return home and to be taken into the business with his father.

For years the war with Spain had dragged on, but now, with the signing of the Treaty of Utrecht, vast new possibilities were opening up of trade to the Americas and a monopoly in the lucrative slave trade to the Spanish colonies. Pryderi was certain he would never want any part of it, such was his own love of the freedom of the open spaces and his love of his fellow man generally.

Although no more interested in politics than in sea-trading, Pryderi had learned during his time in Dublin that there was intrigue everywhere. It was no great surprise when, shortly after his return home, he received a letter from Rupert to say he proposed to call on him. Walking in the garden together Rupert, without preamble, said, 'I have come to you seeking a favour.'

'What sort of favour, Rupert?'

Rupert de Clare paused in his walking.

'We want you,' he said, 'to land a man in Scotland. Your father's ships go that far I believe.'

'Occasionally.'

'I know of no one else to ask. Will you ask your father?'

'Who is the man?'

'That is something I cannot tell you. Except that he is a Frenchman.'

'It's nothing to me,' Pryderi said, 'but you shall stay the night with us and I shall ask him this evening.'

Iestyn Griffiths, however, wanted to know far more of the affair than his easy-going son.

'I don't want to know the name of your Frenchman,' he said, 'but you might like to tell me who I shall be doing it for.'

'That I'm afraid I cannot tell you either, sir,' Rupert said. 'I am sworn to secrecy.'

The older man smiled, 'So it will be Lord Bolingbroke, no doubt.'

Rupert de Clare tried to control his emotions.

'Don't worry,' Iestyn Griffiths said, 'you are a friend of my son's and your secret is safe with me. It is no great mystery. My ships call in many ports and it's my business to know about many things. But can you tell me one good reason why I should give aid to your Lord Bolingbroke?'

'He is a man of high ideals.'

'Is he? He is a Tory, and I am a merchant and a Whig. I am also a Dissenter, as were my people before me. And your precious Lord Bolingbroke has enacted legislation which seeks to destroy us. He is a Protestant.'

'Yes, sir, but he also seeks to put a Catholic back on the throne.'

'For political ends, my boy. No other reason. But this is business. I am no Jacobite. Nor do I have any love for Fat George from Hanover. I'll take your frog-eating friend to Scotland for you as long as the price is right. I'm a Cardi.'

Bolingbroke, however, was too late, for Queen Anne died suddenly. Bolingbroke was outwitted and George of Hanover came to the throne.

Within the year Iestyn Griffiths put the Frenchman ashore on the wild coast of Scotland, and he was there in time for the ill-fated Jacobite rising in support of the Pretender. And that was the sum total of Pryderi's interest in the matter. That same year was momentous for him in another way. It was the great turning point and the answer to all his dreams.

For all their differences of temperament and approach to life, with dissimilar interests, Pryderi and his father were very close, and Iestyn idolised his son.

It was in the early summer of the year of the Jacobite rising that Iestyn Griffiths persuaded Pryderi to accompany him on a voyage to Bristol. His main purpose was to see over a ship of his which was being refitted there in order to carry a more economic cargo of slaves, and he had business to discuss with the master before she sailed. But there was another, less important, reason which appealed immensely to Pryderi. Iestyn had recently made some useful contacts there and was hoping to develop an outlet for thousands of sea-birds' eggs for use in the fining of wines. The sea-birds' eggs would have to come from the islands. And anything to do with the islands was meat and drink to Pryderi.

(3)

Sharp-prowed, and with the wind set fair, the ketch made good time as she ran before the stiff northerly breeze, and the headland of their native coast was soon left far astern to windward. As The Island came in sight Iestyn Griffiths went up to the master and said,

'Could you take her in under The Island, skipper?'

'I've never been in very close before, sir. I've always gave it a wide berth.'

'How does the wind look to you?'

'It be middlin' I'd say, sir, if we can get in under the lee. It's where th'owld Dead Man's Race comes up round the Wolves Teeth as be the nasty part as I've heard tell.'

'The lad is eager to see the place. My old grandmother used to talk to him for hours about it.'

'Well, if you wishes it, sir, and be willin' to risk it.'

'I'll leave it to you, skipper. Take her in quietly and see how she goes.'

Pryderi smiled at his father. Already occasional puffins, guillemots and razorbills were flying across the bows and their numbers increased greatly as they sailed on towards The Island. By the time the pink and white of the cliff-top flowers could be distinguished the birds were everywhere about them in thousands.

'My God, Father. This is something more than Mamgu could ever have described.' The young man was spellbound as he drank in the magic of a scene which all his life he had tried to picture, and his enthusiasm seemed even to affect the captain and his crew. And this was partly responsible for their undoing for, before they knew it, the ketch was swinging into the Dead Man's Race.

'Hard to starboard, Mister,' the captain shouted. But, even as the mate swung the wheel round, the wind backed suddenly and he shouted, 'She won't answer cap'n,' as the sails flapped uselessly.

'Let go the anchor.'

All was now noise and confusion as chains rattled and barefooted seamen sprang to do the captain's bidding. As the anchor caught, the ketch rolled drunkenly into the tide race, the deck cargo buffeted everywhere, then as she swung clear of the Wolves Teeth and came bows up to face the raging current, her cable parted and she bore down helplessly onto The Island's rocks.

(4)

When Iestyn Griffiths walked The Island with his son the following day he saw that fortunate indeed had they been to strike where they had, near a place where they were able to scramble up the cliff quite easily. High and dry, where she was wedged between a jutting rock and the cliff, the ketch had a gaping hole below the waterline.

'She'll never sail again, Father.'

'No, nothing can be more certain than that. But the neap tides are coming on so there'll be a few weeks to salvage a lot of her timber and one thing and another.'

'What'll you do with it?'

'God knows, but let's save what we can. Will you stay with the men?'

'Where are you going?'

'I talked to old Peerce up at the house last night and he's going to take me out tomorrow. I'll get a boat for Bristol and find a new ketch as well. You may as well stay here and do as much as you can.'

'It's all right with the folks up there is it?'

'I've said I'll pay them well. The old man is a decent sort and his housekeeper will do as he says. She's a hardworking young woman and the men can help carry water for her and dig firing and help a bit about the place.'

Pryderi could never have dreamed of such an adventure.

Day after day he was down with the crew, sawing and hammering, and with block and tackle hauling planks and great baulks of timber up the cliff. The furnishings of the vessel, and anything of any value, ropes and chains, sails and shackles were all brought ashore.

Before many days had passed puffins had begun to alight on spars and planks and, bright-eyed and watchful, take an interest in all that was happening.

Jason, the housekeeper's boy, maybe ten years old, full of chatter and with great knowledge of The Island, attached himself to Pryderi and talked incessantly of the birds and the seals, the sheep and the horses and the cattle which he had already begun to herd. One day he took Pryderi to a remote creek and showed him a ketch beneath the water which, he said, became exposed at low spring tides. It had been wrecked there the previous winter and contained a cargo of best roofing slates from the quarries of North Wales. He spoke much of his mother, too, but never was there any mention of a father.

A good-looking woman was Jason's mother, Beth Risman, and, though Pryderi judged her to be at least ten years older than himself, he was greatly attracted to her. Blue-eyed, like himself, she had hair fairer than his own, and her round limbs showed shapely even beneath her simple clothes. From daybreak till after nightfall she was afoot and working hard at cleaning and baking, tending animals, rattling pans and platters in her little dairy, or, after dark, straining her eyes by dim light to stitch and mend at well-worn garments with hands which, though roughened by toil, were yet the finest Pryderi thought he had ever seen. But, though she fed the men well, she spoke little and he sensed a bitterness and a reserve about her with a look in her eyes which he could not fathom. Sometimes it seemed to be of anger and sometimes fear, but always it was guarded.

On odd occasions he had been vaguely conscious of this feeling when the one man of the crew he did not like was near her. A hulking, narrow-eyed, loose-mouthed man he was, lewd of talk and of uncouth manner, and it was of an afternoon when two of the men had gone to the turbary to dig peat for firing and the others to the vessel, that Pryderi, returning for an axe he had forgotten, heard a scream from within the stable.

With the blood pounding in his head as he dashed for the building, some instinct prepared him for what he would find. On a bed of dried fern Beth was fighting wildly against the brute strength of the maniac who pinned her down. Her hair was loosed and the torn front of her garment disclosed the whiteness of her firm breasts.

With a savage oath Pryderi hurled himself on her tormentor and gripped him by the throat. Over they rolled and out onto the cobblestones of the yard as the fight continued. Fingers gouging, knees driving into groins, no word was spoken and deadly was the struggle, blood was on mouths and hands and then Pryderi felt himself being swung aloft, was dimly aware of his head striking something hard and knew no more.

(5)

From the depths of a terrible blackness he felt himself swim giddily towards the light and he knew a cool and gentle touch upon his throbbing brow. Beth Risman was bending over him and in her eyes there was a look of great tenderness such as he had never seen before. He was in a bed in a strange room, but when he would have raised himself his head ached and she stayed him gently with her hand.

'No,' she said, 'bide where you are.' Then she left the room and soon afterwards Pryderi's father came in. Looking down at his son he said, 'Don't you try to talk now. And don't try

to move either. You go back to sleep and I'll be back in a week
or two.' Then he went quietly from the room.

As he slept, Pryderi stirred occasionally, and always he was
conscious of a gentle presence in the room. When at last he
woke, Beth was by the bedside with a cup which held a
sweetly scented brew.

'Drink this,' she said.

He eased himself onto his elbow and she held the cup to his
lips. He pressed her hand gently as he finished it.

Another day passed, but not until the time came when he
was strong enough to be outside in the sunshine was she
willing to talk. Then she said,

'I shall never know how to thank you.'

'He did you no harm?'

'No. But only because you came in time. I could not have
fought him off much longer.'

'What happened?'

'I knew he had been watching me for days but he caught me
unawares. When you pulled him away I ran and called and
called and the captain heard me.'

'What did he do?'

She covered her face with her hands. 'Oh, merciful God.
Brute that he was I never want to see anything like that again
as long as I live. The captain had him lashed to a post, then
stripped him to the waist and had him flogged with a rope.
'Twas sickening to hear him scream and groan before he lost
consciousness.'

'Where is he now?'

'Gone.'

'Gone where?'

'They're all gone. Your father had a new ketch and they've
sailed for Bristol.'

'Dear God, the poor wretch. May the good Lord have
mercy on his soul.'

'You have pity for him?'

'I do indeed. My father will most certainly ship him away
into slavery.'

''Tis a profitable business they say.'

'Yes, my father's made enough profit from it. And from other trading as well. But slavery's a terrible thing, although I've given up trying to protest to him.'

'He worships you.'

'Yes, he's a good father. And the kindest of men in every other way.'

'He has rewarded me very generously for caring for you.'

'I'm glad of that.'

'He pressed five golden guineas on me, which is more than I'm paid for a year's work.'

Of a sudden Pryderi said,

'Why do you work here?'

The guarded look came into her eyes again. 'Does it matter?' she said.

'Yes, to me.'

For a long time she was silent. Then, in a voice not much above a whisper, she said, 'Why did you fight that wretch for me?'

'Wouldn't any man have done the same?'

'No man has ever done as much for me before.'

'Would you have had me stand by whilst you were dishonoured?'

Still in little more than a whisper she said, 'I was dishonoured long ago.'

'Are you talking about Jason?'

'Yes. And he adores you.'

'Who was his father?'

''Twas a big house where I worked. Deceived and betrayed and then turned out. My mother's people came over here years ago with the Flemish weavers. I was a seamstress. But my grandfather came as a soldier with Cromwell and settled here. My father was just as strict and in my shame they would have no more to do with me. Old man Peerce here had lost his wife and was willing to take me in. I've worked hard for what little I get but he's been kind to me. Now he's growing old. His lease finishes this year and when I go back to the mainland I shall be without a home again. Now do you understand what it means to have someone to fight your battles for you?'

For a long time Pryderi was lost in thought. When he spoke it was with a new urgency.

'All my life,' he said, 'I've dreamed of this island. My great-grandmother was brought up here. She ran away with a scoundrel who had been in partnership in a boat with her father but, when he would have robbed and cheated her, she turned to the young captain who had taken over her father's boat. Eventually she married him and they were wonderfully happy and built up a great shipping trade and owned several farms.'

'And you like animals more than ships?'

'I love animals and the land and all living things. I never want to do anything else but farm.'

'Would you have work for me in your house?'

He seemed as if he had not heard her.

'My great-grandmother's people had lived here years before her time. I could be coming home. This could be my house. Why shouldn't I have a lease on it now if the old man is giving up? We could improve the house. We have plenty of timber for a new roof, and doors and floors, and we have a boatload of best slates there for the fetching. We shall need to build a lime-kiln. Father's boats can bring the limestone and culm for burning the lime to improve the pasture. 'Twill be a change from smuggling and landing French agents in Scotland. He's not interested in the Stuart cause, but if the pay is right, it's business. Then we must clear the stones from all these old hutments and use them for walls to make proper field enclosures where we can grow corn and hay instead of having the stock roaming The Island from one end to the other. We could make a wonderful farm of it.'

She smiled at his boyish enthusiasm.

'Why do you say we?'

'Because I mean we.'

'Do you mean you would take me as your housekeeper?'

He coloured as he said, 'No. Would you be willing to marry me instead?'

'I'm much too old for you.'

'How old are you?'

'I'm thirty-two and you're just twenty-one.'

'That wouldn't matter. My great-grandmother used to talk about a princess who had lived here in the once upon a time. Whenever I dreamed of the place I never dreamed there could be a princess here waiting for me. If you could accept one so young. I'll grow out of the fault of being too young daily.'

'But you hardly know me.'

' "Who ever loved that loved not at first sight?" '

'I've heard that saying before. Where does it come from?'

'Shakespeare. But he was quoting Marlowe—

"It lies not in our power to love, or hate,

For will in us is over-ruled by fate.

When two are stripped, long ere the course begin,

We wish that one should lose, the other win;

And one especially do we affect

Of two gold ingots, like in each respect.

The reason no man knows; let it suffice,

What we behold is censured by our eyes.

Where both deliberate their love is slight;

Who ever loved that loved not at first sight?" '

He looked at her earnestly and said, 'The moment I set eyes on you I knew you were the only woman I could ever love.'

Again her voice fell to a whisper.

'Can you mean all these things now you know all there is to know about me?'

He saw the tears in her eyes but, before he could try to rise from where he sat, Jason came towards them round the corner of the house carrying an injured lamb.

(6)

If Iestyn might otherwise have had misgivings, they were considerably allayed by the knowledge of how the young housekeeper had nursed his son and watched over him for hour after weary hour for many days and nights, and he raised no objections. Indeed, he knew how Pryderi's heart had always been in the land and living things, and how avidly as a child he had listened to Mamgu's stories of this Island. The way things had turned out and happened so suddenly it almost seemed as if it had been predestined. So he took it upon himself to arrange for a lease, and Beth sailed up the coast to the Vale of Teify to be married.

By the time young Iestyn, their first child, was born the house had been extended and almost rebuilt, with new floors and roofing timbers and best Caernarvon slates. The beauty of it was that much of the material was already to hand as the result of shipwrecks over the years, and whatever needed to be imported came in one or other of Iestyn's coastal traders.

One of the first priorities had been to build a new limekiln near the top of the track leading up from the beach. Here the limestone was burned with imported anthracite to provide the mortar needed for building the house and the new farm buildings. After that it would be needed for burning lime to fertilise the land. Then there was work to be done clearing the stones of the hutments and compounds of an earlier occupation, using the stones for building field walls. With a vision which marked him as a man ahead of his time Pryderi saw that the whole approach would have to be changed.

Previously, he knew, cattle and sheep had roamed at will all over The Island, so that no hay had been made to feed them through the winter. As a result, stock either had to be sold off for slaughter in the autumn or kept on to lose condition until the following spring. It was wasteful, and it would have to be altered. In the summer it was essential to control the stock. It was one of the earliest lessons he had learned. So, hard work though it meant, walls had to be built. With the salt-laden winds of the Atlantic blowing across The Island in winter there would be no point in trying to plant hedges. All round the coast there was sufficient evidence as to the damage which the burning salt winds could do.

All this meant labour, of course. The farm servants slept in the lofts above the stables and, such was her natural instinct, Beth saw to it that they were well fed. Times for the farming community were not good, and Pryderi's workers, for the most part, appreciated their good fortune.

Whatever Iestyn's initial disappointment may have been when it became clear that Pryderi would never join him in business, now that the die had been cast, he evinced great interest in everything that was happening on The Island and, taking great joy in his baby grandson, lost no opportunity to visit whenever he could. Two cousins had joined him in business.

It was on one of these visits that Iestyn spoke to Pryderi of his plans and discussed what was happening in the outside world. Bolingbroke had been impeached and the Whigs were firmly in control. Lord Stanhope had repealed Bolingbroke's Acts aimed against the Dissenters, so his standing was high with Iestyn Griffiths. And now there were vast possibilities with the trade opening up in the South Seas.

Iestyn told Pryderi that the family had a great deal of money invested in the South Sea Company which carried much of the burden of the National Debt following the Spanish Wars. They had only been drawing interest but there had been a promise that when peace was made the Company would be granted the exclusive right of trade with Spanish South America. It had not worked out like that, however, and now the Company had proposed to the Government that they should hand over the National Debt to them, so that the public creditors would become their shareholders. The proposal was that the Government would only have to pay five percent interest instead of the six or eight percent they were paying to individual creditors. In return the Company were to be granted extended rights to exploit the wealth of South America. So brilliant were the prospects that the company were even proposing to pay the Government a lump sum of seven million pounds over and above the bargain.

Well, of course, Iestyn said, the scheme must be sound because Lord Stanhope had backed it wholeheartedly, and so, as a family company, they were also backing it to the hilt.

In the months which followed, Pryderi had no cause to doubt his father's judgement as news spread through the land of the staggering success of the South Sea Company, and shares were changing hands at astronomically increasing prices. The only two farms on which the Griffiths family did not raise money to buy even more shares were two farms entailed to Pryderi by old great grandma Rhiannon, and there was no time to get to Scalmey to obtain his signature.

Then the crash came. They called it the South Sea Bubble. Lord Stanhope, discredited, died of shock. One of Iestyn's cousins committed suicide, the other left for America, and Iestyn, an old man overnight, was left to pick up the pieces. He died before Walpole took over as Chancellor of the Exchequer, and salvaging something from the wreckage, managed to pay creditors thirty-three percent.

(7)

Sad though he was at the loss of his father, and though he missed his visits and the interest he had taken, Pryderi did not consider himself to be any worse off financially than before the disaster. He still had his two farms, there was what was to come to him when everything of his father's estate had been settled, and the bulk of the expense for establishing a sound farm on The Island had already been met.

Jason, having been much interested in Iestyn's ketches when they came to The Island, showed an inclination to go to sea, and Pryderi ensured that one good ketch was saved for him. Pryderi had already taught him to read and write.

With no more interest in politics than in his younger days as a student, Pryderi, even so, remembered something of his father's comments and observations over the years. He remembered his saying how violently Lord Stanhope and Viscount Townshend had disagreed, so when Townshend retired from politics to concentrate on farming his estate in Norfolk, Pryderi was interested. As the years went by he followed news of Turnip Townshend's pioneering work and his own farming benefitted from it.

Out of respect to his father's memory, following his death, Pryderi instituted the custom of morning and evening prayers for the family. There were three more, a boy and two girls, to follow the first grandson whom Iestyn had adored. And on Sunday mornings Pryderi began to include the servants in the morning prayer, and the custom was to remain until the end of his life.

On one occasion he made one of his rare visits to his native county to attend to business concerning one of the two farms he still owned and, staying over the week-end, he heard Daniel Rowlands of Llangeitho, in the neighbouring Vale of Aeron, preach. It was the monthly communion service and there, in the open air, there must have been a thousand people partaking. Rowlands' fame as one of the great Revivalists had spread through the land. A churchman originally, who had actually been vicar of Llangeitho, he had become one of John Wesley's Methodists. Like all good Dissenters he rallied against the papists, but Pryderi could not believe that what he had to say applied to his friend of youth, Rupert de Clare, or others of the same persuasion he had met at that time. Pryderi's philosophy in life had always been one of live and let live. It was perhaps this, as well as affection for his father's memory, which influenced him when one of his father's old friends spoke to him that same week-end of the difficulties they had with all their services having to be conducted in the open air.

So it was that Pryderi Griffiths, Esquire, of Scalmey, endowed a new chapel in his native land. But he thought his own thoughts about the narrowness of much that he had heard, and sailed home thankfully to the care-free life of his Island fastness and the warmth and love of Beth and his family.

(8)

When Pryderi thought of his own love of the land and livestock he thought back to his herdsman ancestor on The Island all those years ago and recognized that it was in his blood, or reverting to type, as some folks called it. And now

Iestyn, his and Beth's first son, wanted nothing more from life than to sail the seas and see the world, and in this he was encouraged by the letters which came now and again from Jason.

The boy's keeness gave Pryderi to think what a disappointment he may have been to his own father, with his steadfast refusal to show any interest in the business, and his determination to go his own way. And he remembered how, in spite of it, when the time came, his father had encouraged and supported him in every way he could, and the interest he had shown right up to the end. So Pryderi showed the same interest and encouraged his son.

At various times of the year farmers came to The Island to buy cattle or corn and it was perhaps no surprise that, in the fullness of time, the two girls should have met farmers' sons and married them.

But the last and youngest, Owen, was Pryderi all over again. From first thing in the morning until sleepy-eyed bedtime, he was about the buildings and the fields, wherever the animals were. In the spring he was there on the cliff-tops to see the first puffin come to land and, by an early age, he knew every species of sea-bird that came to the great cliffs, and he knew the different names by which they had been known over the passing years. He came to know the migratory birds of autumn, too, and, when the woodcock came in great numbers, he began to take an interest in game birds and to observe the flighting habits of the wild duck that frequented the ponds and fed on the corn stubble in late summer.

So it was, in the spring of the year when Owen was fifteen, Pryderi planned a surprise for him and sent to a gamekeeper he knew on the mainland for a sitting of pheasants' eggs.

Owen was intrigued when the eggs arrived and they put the hen to sit. That was no new experience for him. He had the box turned on its side facing the wall for the hen to have a bit of peace and quiet, and he placed an upturned sod of earth in the bottom to keep the eggs moist. They knew from experience that the broody hen they had was one that sat tight and was a good mother. His father had told him he had sent for a special sitting of hens' eggs, but when he saw the fifteen pale olive eggs he knew they were something different.

He looked at them for a long time and then, his blue eyes wrinkling in a knowing smile, said, 'Are they pheasants' eggs, Father?'

'I shouldn't wonder,' Pryderi said. 'I shouldn't wonder one bit.'

'How long will they take to hatch?'

'A bit longer than a hen.'

'Longer?'

'Just a couple of days.'

Blodwen, Owen called the hen, and he tended her faithfully, putting food and water when she left the nest, and sprinkling the eggs with water towards the end of the incubation.

Then, after an eternity, which seemed far, far longer than two days over the three weeks, the first shell cracked and, within twenty-four hours, twelve of the fifteen eggs had hatched.

Rearing the chicks was easy. No rats or foxes were there on The Island, and it was no great task to protect a pen to save them from the occasional hawk. As they grew, and their feathers came, it was seen that fortune was continuing to smile, for seven of the young birds were hens and five were cocks.

'We'll pick the best two cocks for turning out with the hens,' Pryderi said, 'and we'll keep the other three in and fatten them for Christmas.'

'How is that then, Father?'

'Well if you have too many cocks they'll start fighting over the hens on the nests and smash the eggs. One cock to three or four hens is plenty. And in a year or two when they've started to breed and you can start shooting, make sure you shoot more cocks than hens. Always leave plenty of hens, for they're the ones to breed. Remember what it says in the Bible, ''If a bird's nest chance to be before thee in the way in any tree, or on the ground, whether they be young ones, or eggs, and the dam sitting upon the young, or upon the eggs, thou shalt not take the dam with the young; But thou shalt in anywise let the dam go, and take the young to thee; that it may be well with thee, and that thou mayest prolong thy days.'' And next year we'll have some partridge eggs.'

So, with talk of shooting, it was time for Owen to have his first lessons in the handling and management of a gun. He would also need a dog.

From as far back as he could remember his constant companion had been Ianto, the brave Cardiganshire dog of the cowhouse. Corgis they called them. Red like a fox he was, with a bushy tail like a fox, but he had a white chest and four white feet, and never could there have been a more faithful dog anywhere in all the world. But even brave and faithful companions cannot live for ever and, back in the winter, Ianto grew old and died. Owen tried to be brave, too, like Ianto had always been brave, so nobody saw his tears, for he went round to the back of the stables to shed them. Ianto had been replaced as a working dog. After a fashion. There was a young dog of sorts romping about the place, but nobody could ever find a place like Ianto had always had in Owen's heart. Or so Owen thought. Until Teify came.

He called him Teify because he came to them from the Vale of Teify where his father had been born and brought up. A tarfgi Teify was. The dog for flushing the birds up out of the marshy ground. The dog for scattering them. So that's why they called them tarfgis up there. But down here where they spoke no Welsh they called them springer spaniels.

Red and white Teify was. And, even as a puppy the lovely, gentle nature of him was there for anyone to see in his adoring, brown eyes. Then, when he grew on his feathered legs, with his ears set low, and his sharp head alert to all about him, had there ever been a springer spaniel to compare with him since they had been referred to in the Laws of Hywel Dda almost a thousand years ago? Faithful and affectionate, he loved to please, to learn and to obey. Hunting through the swedes and turnips, or working the corn stubbles or marshy ground, his quivering tail told of his excitement and the sheer joy he had in being alive.

When Owen began at last to shoot, never once did Teify allow a winged bird to remain unfound. And when he retrieved a bird, so gentle was his velvet mouth that never a mark did he leave on it. Hard though it was for him at first, he even learned that he must never be sidetracked from the main business of life by chasing rabbits. For the rabbits were caught every winter by rabbit catchers who came across from the mainland with their ferrets and nets and a couple of lurchers.

(9)

As the years went by and Teify joined Ianto in his last, long sleep, there were other corgis and there were other tarfgis. But never, for Owen, could there be another corgi like Ianto or another tarfgi like Teify.

Owen married and brought his bride to live on The Island and they were blessed with children.

And then Pryderi and Beth grew old. More than fifty years they had shared together. Jason, married to a girl he had met in an English port, had prospered. Iestyn, too, had prospered, although he had not married. And the two girls had prospered. And farming was doing better.

In the spring the birds came, as they had always come. As they always did, Pryderi and Beth strolled in the warmth of the afternoon, to look again at the first puffins with the eternal promise of new life, and to count their blessings.

Often in their walks little Daniel, their grandson, came with them. He adored his Gamp Preedy. Gamp it had been at first, but then he heard Gran call him Pryderi, and so he became Gamp Preedy. Pryderi was more than Daniel could manage. So, Gamp Preedy it remained. But now, at ten years old, Daniel was growing more boisterous and active, with new interests, and, today the men were gathering the sheep and Daniel had to be with them. They agreed obligingly they could not manage without Daniel, so Pryderi and Beth strolled to the cliff-tops on their own.

Together on the close-cropped sward they sat in silence. No need was there for great talk, for close indeed was the bond of companionship between them. Everywhere around them was a vastness of blue, from the depths of the crystal clear sea, way out to the far horizon and soaring above to the unfathomable infinity of the sky. Sloops, ketches and, further out, great barques and schooners, ploughed their white foaming wakes under full sails and a fair wind.

On the ledges the guillemots and razorbills were already jostling for position in a great, groaning macrocosm. Soon now the fishermen would be coming from the mainland to go down the great cliffs on ropes for the seasonal harvest of eggs. On the greensward sloping to the cliff-tops the clown-like puffins bobbed and curtsied and croaked and shot in and out of the rabbit burrows which they had come to commandeer for their breeding season. Way up in the haze of the blue heights a pair of larks were pouring out their joyful carol. Pryderi and Beth were at peace. And then, at last, Pryderi spoke.

'How old are you now, Beth?' he said.

'You shouldn't ask a lady that. But it's eighty seven I'll be this summer.'

'Not really?'

'True. And you'll be seventy six.'

'And you're still as lovely as ever.'

'Do you really think so?'

He squeezed her hand and said, 'Do you think you made a big mistake? Marrying one so young?'

'Yes, you're starting to wheeze and puff a bit. But it's too late to change my mind now.'

All the way as they strolled back to the house they held hands as they always did when they walked. But it was the last time for them to see the puffins.

Hardly did they know on The Island what it was to have a cold, unless somebody went to the mainland and came back with one. And that was what happened in the autumn.

Pryderi had never been ill in his life, but now he took to his bed and he sweat. Beth dosed him, and kept him well covered, and sat with him as he became delirious and then lost consciousness. For three days and three nights she had not closed her eyes, but she was still with him in the cold light of dawn when he breathed his last.

She went to her chair then in the corner by the fire and they prevailed on her to drink some broth.

She slept at last, so they tip-toed from the room and left her.

She was still sleeping when they tip-toed to look at her in the afternoon. It was a lovely sleep she was having, for the gentle smile on her face said so. Her lifeless hands were in her lap and one of them held the bracelet.

Chapter 6

War With France

(1)

When Daniel's son was born it was not surprising that he should have been named Preedy. Daniel wanted him named after his grandfather, Pryderi, whom he had adored. But, as he had always called the old man Gamp Preedy, if the idea was to name the baby after him, then it seemed only natural to name him Preedy. So Preedy it was.

Preedy, however, when he was of an age to take interest and an active part in the shaping of the family fortunes, knew little of the hardships and struggles which those before him had been forced to endure, for the wars with France were about to begin all over again. Eventually there was a duty on corn, it paid handsomely to grow it at home, and as much land as possible was turned over by the plough. Farming fortunes were recovering to some purpose.

Old Uncle Iestyn had outlived his younger brother Owen, Daniel's father, and had come to The Island to end his days, as he put it. But, at close on eighty years, he seemed as spry as ever, and, although he advised caution, his eyes lit up when Daniel talked of the possibility of buying a smack.

'The good times won't last for ever, mind,' he said. 'When the war is over they'll soon be shouting for cheap food again. And 'tis a risky business trying to keep a smack here. 'Tis no place to keep a boat like that.'

''Twould be useful though, Uncle Iestyn, growing so much corn to have a smack of our own.'

So they talked about it for some time, and then Uncle Iestyn, seeing that Daniel was determined, said he would write to old Henry Adams, a famous boat-builder of Buckler's Hard in Hampshire.

'He's given up now,' Uncle Iestyn said, 'and his sons have taken over. But I've known Henry on and off for years, and if there's anything going he'll know.'

There was something else in Uncle Iestyn's mind as well. Years ago his half-brother Jason, when in port at Lymington, had picked up with a girl there, married her and finally settled down to live in the area. Iestyn had kept in touch with them over the years, but felt a little guilty that he had heard nothing for some time. And he felt this the more keenly because, when Jason died and, not long afterwards, his son was lost at sea, Iestyn had taken it upon himself to become a sort of guardian to the family. It must have been all of ten years since he had last played with little, fair-haired and blue-eyed Beth Sawyer, Jason's great-grand-daughter. Named after Jason's mother she had been. Beth, who had died peacefully in her chair with a smile on her face and the bracelet in her lap. But the bracelet had been handed down to Pryderi's children, which was as it should be, because it was from his family it had come. And young Beth Sawyer must be growing up now and just about as old as young Preedy.

'We'll sail up the Bewley river to Buckler's Hard,' said Uncle Iestyn, 'and it won't take me long to slip across to Lymington from there.' That was the day he heard at last from old Henry Adams. His boys, he said, were only building big ships now, but there was a thirty-eight ton smack, the Dancing Dervish, one of the last he had built ten years previously, which was just in for a complete re-fit. As an old friend he strongly recommended her, said she was as good as new and could probably be bought for not much more than five hundred pounds.

(2)

The voyage in search of the Dancing Dervish, Preedy, at sixteen years of age, regarded as more momentous than anything that had ever happened in his life previously. And that was before he could know anything of all that was to befall before they were to sail home proudly more than a fortnight later.

It was evident from the start that Uncle Iestyn was a well-known, much respected, member of a great maritime brotherhood. All three generations went. Preedy, Daniel and Uncle Iestyn. And Uncle Iestyn contrived to get them a passage, without charge, on a great schooner, which picked them up at sea from a small coastal trader. The schooner was bound for Southampton water. Bigger by far she was than anything on which Preedy had ever been before and, unused to the great, surging roll, he was sick most of the way, and remembered little of the voyage.

Words had never been invented to describe his relief as they transferred to a dandy which, he discovered later, had been built at Cardigan, and sailed up the Bewley river. Beautiful the country was, but with a beauty quite different from the grandeur of his native cliffs.

It was early in the month of February, in the year 1797, and the wild geese and the wild duck at the water's edge made a thrilling sight. Curlew they had on The Island. They bred there and Preedy loved their haunting call, so he recognised them easily. But other waders there were which he had never seen before and he had no idea what their names were.

Where the fields ran down to the water's edge there was a feeling of great peace. Elsewhere the slopes were clothed with trees which, Preedy imagined, must be truly beautiful when they wore their full dress. Never in his life, and certainly not on windswept Scalmey, had he seen such trees. Then, as they sailed on in the dawn light, the peace was broken by the bustling activity of what he knew must be Buckler's Hard. Uncle Iestyn had told him enough for him to recognise it. One great ship towering above them on her stocks was ready for launching. Thirty-eight guns she was to carry, and she was to be named the Boadicea. Three other big ships were also under construction.

The dandy, heading up-river for a cargo of bricks from the thriving brickyard at Bailey's Hard, put them ashore, and they made their way to the Ship Inn for a bite to eat. Then Uncle Iestyn went in search of Henry Adams. A fine old gentleman he was, with a strong face, and he was obviously greatly knowledgeable about ships. By mid-day he had produced a crew from somewhere and they were aboard the

Dancing Dervish. As Uncle Iestyn took the helm, and they headed down river, he was smiling.

Not until they reached the open sea did he call orders to the crew in strange nautical terms, as the ship altered course, plied on and off, and tacked again. Then finally, they put about, and Iestyn winked and nodded at Daniel and said, 'She'll do. She'll do.' Then he called Preedy to him and stood by him as he took the wheel.

They moored at Buckler's Hard, the deal was struck before nightfall, and they slept on board the Dancing Dervish that night. There was still some work to be done, but they would be ready to sail for home in a few days. Henry Adams knew two men who would be willing to sign on as crew for the voyage, and Iestyn proposed to spend the days whilst waiting seeking for some word of young Beth.

(3)

Preedy found the red brick houses of Buckler's Hard quite different from the white-limed and pink-washed cottages of the mainland at home. And here, instead of the familiar thatched roofs, there were warm and solid red tiles. In the wide village street there were great stacks of massive timbers, and there was an air of bustling prosperity. Yet the people, although friendly, were quiet and slow spoken.

It was in the evening one or two of them began to talk when Preedy went with his father and Uncle Iestyn to the Ship Inn. The talk was friendly and those who did not speak to them showed no interest. It was a seafaring place where many strangers came and went. They had been doing business with Mr Adams and that was a warranty of their good standing.

At different tables in the dim-lit tavern various people seemed to be conducting business. Where there was open talk it was of the latest news of the war with the French, and of developments at Buckler's Hard. The opinion was expressed that the Adams sons were building too many big ships and were over-reaching themselves. Through the haze of taboccao smoke Preedy saw two seafaring men come in

through the door and go to the bar. He knew they were
sailors from their striped jerseys and flat, round hats. They
paid for the tankards of ale they ordered and moved with
their rolling gait towards the bench in the far corner.

Iestyn exchanged a look with the man behind the bar, who
nodded almost imperceptibly. Iestyn got up and went over to
the two sailors. For a few minutes he talked to them quietly,
then they came back with him to the table where Preedy and
his father were sitting.

Their faces were weather-beaten and their hands calloused. One of them had an old scar running down from his
eye to his mouth, yet contrived to look cheerful in spite of it.
Somewhere in their forties Preedy judged them to be. The
one with the scar was called Charlie Wigan. Whether that
was his real name, or whether he was known as that because
he came from Wigan, Preedy never discovered. But they
discovered straightaway that he was anxious to get back
there.

'Ship were sunk,' he said. 'Bloody mounseers. I were reet
lucky to be picked up. Only six on us left from a crew of o'er
fifty. Tek us to Cardigan mister an' I'll get ship from theer.
Theer's misus an' three kids wonderin' what's happened.'

So the conversation went, but it was not until much later
that his mate, Jem Burlace, came to the point. He, like
Charlie Wigan, was only signing on for the trip and reckoned
on finding a vessel on which he could work his passage back
to Lymington. He was a native. And he knew the name of
Iestyn Griffiths as one to be trusted.

'You see mister, us do be careful. Ar, us do need to be that,'
he said.

'Who d'you call us?' Iestyn asked. 'Just as if I didn't know.
Are you in with the Gentlemen?'

Jem Burlace permitted himself the barest hint of a knowing
smile.

'What's the deal?'

Burlace thought for a few moments. 'Brandy?' he said.

Iestyn and Daniel exchanged glances.

'Could be,' Iestyn said. 'What else?'

'Tobacco? Silk?'

'Could be,' Iestyn said again, 'How much?'

'For the Dervish it 'ud be a whole cargo.'

'Jesus! You're asking us to risk something aren't you?'

'Us got to shift it. The Gentlemen can't touch it.'

'Where is it?'

'Over to Chewton Bunny.'

'So what's the trouble? Don't tell me you're worried about the preventive men?'

'Sojers. The Dragoons. Reckons as there be a spy from the mounseers landed at Hurst Castle. The place be a swarmin' with sojers. Happen they don't catch nobody 'twon't be long awhile afore they reaches Chewton Bunny. Us daresn't run it inland, but us'll ha' to shift it.'

Iestyn and Daniel exchanged another glance. For the first time Daniel spoke. He said, 'You won't be asking too high a price then will you?'

Jem Burlace concealed his thoughts well. 'You'll never get yourself a cheaper cargo, mister,' was all he said.

'Who do we deal with?' Iestyn said.

'Be at the Queen's Head at Burley tomorrow night.'

(4)

It was no more than a dozen miles to Burley, but Iestyn needed to go Lymington way to enquire about Beth. In the couple of days Uncle Iestyn would be away Daniel would try to hasten forward the final work which still needed to be done before the Dancing Dervish sailed. Iestyn was reckoning to sail on the Thursday in time to make Chewton Bunny by nightfall. He had been gone scarcely an hour when Preedy discovered they had a stowaway. A ginger tomcat he was, in fine fettle except insofar as he had lost one eye. Not surprisingly subsequent enquiries established that his name was Nelson, after the sailor who had lost his eye at Calvi, about the same time as this feline namesake was losing his in a rather less illustrious encounter with another ginger tom even more fearsome than himself. Nelson, however, had

managed to relieve his protagonist of one ear. Now, he
attached himself to Preedy and demanded to be fed. His
hunger and thirst having been assuaged he disappeared. It
was the two carpenters working on the vessel who were able
to tell of his name and history. They seemed to know him well
by repute and said the only time he was seen was either when
he wanted feeding or when there was some excitement.

The carpenters had finished and left the smack on the
Wednesday, but it was Friday morning before Iestyn
returned. When he came across the gangplank, carrying a
bundle, Preedy's heart jumped, for there came with him a
lovely fair-haired girl of about Preedy's own age who was the
prettiest girl he had ever seen. When he thought about it, it
detracted nothing from her beauty that he had seen very few
girls in his life anyway.

It was much later that Uncle Iestyn had time to tell of how
he had found her, homeless and forlorn, and of the mishaps
which had befallen her family over the years. For the
moment it was a case of all hands on deck in preparation for
sailing. Charlie Wigan and Jem Burlace had already come
aboard.

There was a small cabin which Uncle Iestyn and Daniel
agreed should be for Beth, and Preedy was glad she would
have some privacy. And Daniel had said without being
asked, that there would be a home for her on The Island.
'She's family isn't it?' he said. 'And that's what it's all about,
like.'

Uncle Iestyn took Preedy to one side then and, from a
locker produced two murderous looking pistols which he
concealed about his person. Then he produced a belt and a
seaman's knife far more wicked and murderous looking than
the pistols.

'Please God,' Uncle Iestyn said, 'we won't need 'em. But
I've been all over and I've stayed alive sometimes by being
ready, trusting nobody and not taking any more chances
than I had to.'

Preedy fastened the belt round his waist and fingered the
awesome, razor sharpness of the knife with its deadly point.

'You've heard tell of the great Owen Griffiths,' Uncle Iestyn said. 'One of our ancestors way back. That knife belonged to him. He defended a young woman's honour with it and he marked a bad man for life with it.'

'What d'you expect to happen, Uncle Iestyn?'

'Nothing, I hope. But I've told you before I've stayed alive by being prepared. Until we get home there'll always be two of us awake and on watch at the same time. Either you and me, you and your father, or me and your father.'

Preedy made up a rough bunk for himself near the door to Beth's cabin. He knew already he would die for her if need be.

When their stores had been safely stowed, and they were ready to sail, Beth announced that she had prepared a rough meal in the galley. And it was there that Uncle Iestyn told them his news.

'Last night,' he said, 'I met Ianto Pugh, a seaman from Cardigan. He'd just come ashore and had met one of the Breton crabbers. They're part of France, in a way, but there's no love lost between 'em. The crabbers sail from a place called Camaret. And Ianto had news from the crabber that there's three French warships and a lugger just arrived at Brest ready to sail from Camaret. It's part of the froggies' invasion plan that went wrong at Bantry Bay at Christmas. This time they're planning to take Bristol by surprise and set fire to the city.'

'When do they sail?' Charlie Wigan asked.

'That I don't know. But if their plans are that well-known it could be any day. So we can reckon to keep our weather eye open and not hang about.'

'Ianto Pugh,' Daniel said. 'Is he reliable?'

'As true as they come. He's been doing trade with the Gentlemen. He'll be there tonight when we take our cargo on board and he'll sail with us. We'll be glad of the extra hand.'

Preedy caught the glance which his father and Uncle Iestyn exchanged and he guessed what they were thinking. Should there be trouble they would have one more ally. And with such an ally there could be less likelihood of trouble.

(5)

As they set sail and the Dancing Dervish, without ballast, leaned over gently in the breeze, Preedy felt a sense of elation. He knew she would would be steadier when they had taken their cargo on board.

The plan was to heave-to at a stretch known as Fiddler's Reach and take one of Jem Burlace's confederates on board. It would not have been wise for him to have been seen at Buckler's Hard. The preventive men had their eyes everywhere.

Sure enough, as they hove-to, a skiff with a man seated in the stern-sheets came out from somewhere along the shore and, almost before Preedy realised what was happening, the man had swarmed up the rope ladder which Jem Burlace had lowered for him, and the Dancing Dervish was under way again. Uncle Iestyn called Preedy over to him at the wheel and said, 'Learn as much as you can now whilst you've got the chance. You never know when it might come in useful.'

The wind, not too fresh, was from the east so that, once out in the Solent, they were able to run with it, but the wind was cold and Preedy's fingers stung. As they cleared the point at Hurst Castle the low light came on. By the time they were off Highcliffe, darkness had fallen.

'Couldn't have timed it better,' Uncle Iestyn said.

Jem Burlace's confederate produced a latern which he lit. Of an odd shape it was, with the only light it gave coming from a long spout at the side. Beth had come to stand at Preedy's side.

'Now 'ee do know what a smuggler's lantern be,' she said. He loved the way she spoke.

Already a companionship had sprung up between them, but there had been little chance to talk to her. Certainly there would be even less chance for the next dozen hours or so, for a hard night's work lay ahead of them.

The signal from the lantern was immediately answered by a dim light from the shore. At Iestyn's suggestion Jem Burlace took the wheel. It was eerie moving in to where they could hear the breakers under the cliffs in the darkness and then, at a nod from Jem Burlace, Uncle Iestyn shouted, 'Let go th'anchor.'

A rattling of chain, the mainsail swung free, and more brief signals from the lanterns were exchanged. Minutes later the dim shape of a heavy rowing boat could be faintly discerned coming alongside, and then a short, broad-shouldered man came up over the rail, and Preedy somehow knew it was Ianto Pugh. Two more men followed him and it soon became obvious that there would, at least, be no shortage of hands to help stow the cargo of barrels and bales.

Suddenly, without any warning, Preedy felt a warmth brushing against his leg and then, tail erect, Nelson stalked across the deck to observe and, so it seemed, to supervise.

Three rowing boats there were, and no sooner would one return to shore than another, full-laden, would take its place. All through the night, as the wind freshened and blew colder, the great basket on the spar fixed to the mast swung out and down and was hoisted up by means of a pulley. Out and down, a low murmur, and hoist it up. Slow work it was, but almost monotonously the basket was swung out and down to be hoisted back up again. And steadily the holds of the smack began to fill.

Preedy, with Beth never far from his side, marvelled at the easy efficiency of it all. Shadowy figures moved to and fro across the deck, and down below dim lights burned low. Tramp of feet, thump of barrel and bale, but scarce a word all night. The moon was at the full, but it was a night of heavy cloud which, Iestyn said, was just as well. There was plenty of light for them to see what they were doing.

By daybreak the holds were full, the hatches fastened down, and the Dancing Dervish was ready to continue on her way.

The entire operation having apparently been completed to his satisfaction, Nelson marched off, tail still erect, to disappear in the direction of the dark places below deck.

(6)

Uncle Iestyn and Preedy took first turn at the helm. The old man was anxious to see how the smack handled, now that she was laden, and he soon declared himself satisfied. Then he stood by Preedy as he took over at the wheel.

Still from the east, the breeze continued strong, and the Dancing Dervish drove on before it like a greyhound. Preedy thrilled at the sight of the great sails towering above them and the sound of the wind whistling in the taut stays. Yet he knew that Uncle Iestyn was on edge. More than once had he chafed at having been a day late sailing.

Eventually Ianto Pugh came to stand by them and said, 'More serious it is than ever I thought Iestyn.'

'The froggies?'

'Diawl, aye. The mounseers.'

No chance had they had for any such talk all through the night as they loaded their contraband with a fierce determination to be through with their task by first light out of sight of prying eyes.

'What more have you heard?' Iesyn asked.

'The word is, bach, that they're sailing tonight.'

'Tonight? Who'd know a thing like that?'

'I crossed in the same ship as the mounseer's spy. Put him drunk we did. They've got an Irish American in charge. Colonel William Tate. Ever heard of him, Iestyn?'

'Yes. A tough nut. Made his name in the War of Independence. From Carolina.'

'Diawl, aye. That's the one. And his orders if he can't make Bristol is to land in Cardigan Bay.'

'Cardigan?'

'Yes indeed. Cardigan whatever. And he won't take Bristol by surprise for word have been sent there already.'

'What about the froggy?'

'Duw, duw bach. Let him go they did. He's being followed closer than a hen with one chicken. See who his contact is. So Cardigan it'll be for the mounseers by the look of it, and that's why I was so keen to come with you.'

Iestyn looked up at the steel blue sky and away to the white caps on the distant waves. Then he sniffed the wind and said, 'If this blow keeps up from that quarter I doubt if they'll ever make Bristol.'

'Then bad it'll be for our folks round Cardigan whatever. They've got nearly two thousand soldiers aboard and half of 'em convicts let out for the job.'

'What's the idea of that then, Ianto?'

'Land 'em and get rid of 'em I shouldn't wonder isn't it? If they don't do nothing else they'll play hell all round the countryside for a spell.'

'How much d'you know about the French ships?'

'Two of the biggest and newest frigates in the mounseers' navy. Forty guns apiece. And there's a twenty-four gun corvette and a fourteen gun lugger just come back from Bantry Bay. There's a Commodore Castagnier in charge. Another tough man back from the American War. Privateer.'

'How sure can you be they'll sail tonight?'

Ianto puckered his low brow, and his brown eyes looked keenly at Iestyn.

'Diawl, bach, how can we be sure?'

'But if they do sail tonight shall we make Land's End ahead of them?'

'Duw, duw, Iestyn. You do know better than me.'

'But what do you think? I know what I think.'

'What's that, Iestyn bach?'

'I think we'll be better off ahead of 'em if we can keep to windward of 'em than if we fall behind.'

'The way she's sailing now whatever, I reckon we'll make the Wolf Rock by tomorrow morning,' Ianto said.

'And the froggies won't make it much before that.'

'If they do sail tonight.'

'If they sail tonight. If.'

By the time Preedy went below to sleep at last they had cleared Portland Bill without mishap by keeping well out, and the coast was receding from view. His father had come to relieve him and said that Beth had a meal for him in the galley. He and Jem Burlace and Charlie Wigan had already eaten.

Preedy would have talked to her but, with the warmth of the galley after the bitter cold of the biting east wind, he suddenly realised how tired he was. The night's tension and excitement had kept him awake, and then had come the thrill of handling the Dancing Dervish carried before such a following wind, but now his head began to nod and his eyes to close. Beth had gone to her little cabin before he finished, and scarcely could he remember falling onto his own rough bunk before he was unaware of the gentle lift and fall and the bumping of the water against stout timbers as the vessel surged on.

Darkness had fallen by the time he came back on deck and his father was at the wheel with Ianto Pugh. The moon, which had been hidden by heavy cloud the previous night, was now laying a rippling swath of silver across the endless expanse of ocean.

'Where are we, Father?' Preedy asked.

'We're back in the land of the living then? Last time I looked at you I didn't think you'd ever speak again.'

'Oh, good God, I've slept! Where are we?'

'Have you ever heard of Start Point?' Ianto asked.

'Where's that then?'

'Well if you haven't heard of it, bach, you won't see it neither. We've passed it.'

Preedy looked round, but all he beheld was infinity. Then Uncle Iestyn joined them.

'Sleep well?' Daniel said.

'Like a new born babbie,' said Iestyn.

'We'll turn in then,' Ianto Pugh said, 'any sign of grub down below?'

'Beth is sleeping,' Preedy said.

'Leave her be, then,' Daniel said, 'she've done more than her share. We'll have something when we wake.'

Then, once more, Preedy and the old man were alone at the wheel together. Ahead of them a light appeared and Uncle Iestyn said, 'We're making good time, boy. That's the Eddystone. 'Tis a fine lighthouse. Pity you didn't see it on the way up. But you weren't in a fit state to look at anything.'

Preedy laughed, 'That old big ship was too much for me.'

'You'd get used to it in time. But the Eddystone was only built about forty years ago. Wonderful piece of work. The old one was made of wood and burnt down. Did you ever hear about it?'

'No I didn't.' Preedy loved to listen to the old man's tales of his voyages all over the world.

'We sailed past when it was burning, but there was nothing anybody could do. There was an old man about eighty or ninety in charge of the light and the other two chaps with him were drunk. The fire started up above and crept down. The old man was looking up and had his mouth open and some molten lead went straight down into his stomach and he didn't feel a thing. Or so he said.'

'Is that true, Uncle Iestyn?' Preedy had never known the old man to be a teller of tall stories.

'Aye, well, nobody believed him, of course. Bill Hall his name was. By the time the fire was finished they were out on the rocks and eventually a boat got 'em off. Poor old Bill Hall died about twelve days after, and out of curiosity the doctor opened him up. And sure enough there was a half pound lump of lead inside him.'

For the rest of the uneventful night, with the Dancing Dervish sailing steadily, Preedy, well wrapped against the cold, listened to the old man's fascinating reminiscences. At daybreak Uncle Iestyn took his telescope and scanned the horizon to the south, but nothing could he see to cause alarm.

By mid-day they were north of the Wolf Rock and had set course for Land's End. Preedy was taking a turn with the spyglass, resting it on the rail, and it was he who saw, far astern and to the south-west of the Wolf Rock, the top-masts of what must be three big ships.

Daniel was at the wheel, and Uncle Iestyn and Ianto were below.

'What are those then, Father?' Preedy said and beckoned to Jem Burlace and Charlie Wigan who were on deck.

It was Charlie, taking the spy-glass, who said, 'Eh, lad, I'll tell thee, that's mounseers reet enough. Reckon I've seen their riggin' before now. Best give t'owld chap a shout.'

Roused from their brief sleep Uncle Iestyn and Ianto hurried on deck, and then Beth joined them.

'What do we do now?' Daniel said. Preedy exchanged looks with Beth. She smiled, and he knew fear. He had never thought of himself as a coward, and he knew that the fear was for Beth.

As if voicing Preedy's thoughts Ianto said, 'Fall foul of that lot whatever and there's no hope for any of us.' He, too, glanced at Beth and exchanged a troubled look with Iestyn.

'Right then,' Iestyn said resolutely, 'we'll have to beat it for the Bristol Channel. Full and by it is. And then, it'll be close-hauled all the way to keep to windward of 'em.'

There was authority in every word, and the three of them moved swiftly to do his bidding. Preedy marvelled at their quick, practiced movements and, watching the unquestioning attitude of Jem Burlace and Charlie Wigan, smiled at the thought that they could have had any doubts about them. The danger was coming from an unexpected quarter. And, come to think of it, old Uncle Iestyn had been preparing for that as well, chafing at the lost day and, all the time, calculating where the French vessels might be, and what action could be taken, in the various contingencies.

By the time the light was fading the hulls of the warships could be seen above the horizon, and the lugger had come into view as well. Tail erect, Nelson emerged from below to stalk the deck.

Preedy was at the wheel. Standing alongside him, Uncle Iestyn said, 'If ever you've prayed in your life, boy, pray now that the wind'll stay where 'tis. Tomorrow will be the test. Keep your eyes up there to the top of the sail and keep her as close to the wind as ever she'll go. Just the tiniest flicker in the corner below the gaff. Tomorrow you'll see the froggies overhauling us something cruel, but we'll sail five points closer to the wind than ever they will.'

And then, all through the night, they were driving ahead in the cold light of the moon. A different story it was now, with the wind in their faces, the spray flying as the Dancing Dervish drove into the swell, sometimes, bows under, with her foredeck awash, but never so much as giving the slightest sign of faltering. Little rest was there for anybody that night and Beth, brave soul, came to them all in turn, albeit unsteadily, with bread and cheese and steaming toddy.

When daybreak came they could see the high shape of Lundy rising out of the sea ahead of them, and the four black-sided French vessels closing in on them astern. But old Iestyn smiled grimly and Preedy could see that they were well in the lee of their own small craft.

Ianto it was who had the spy-glass. At last he said, 'Well, Iesu mawr, they're flyin' white ensigns.'

'Never!' Iestyn said.

'Here, bach, see for yourself then isn't it.'

Iestyn took the spy-glass and then looked at Ianto and smiled.

'Well, by damn,' he said.

As they watched, a small cutter could be seen sailing towards the Frenchmen. Doubtless those aboard had been puzzled by the British flags flying at the ensign staffs and were intent on taking a closer look.'

'We'll soon see,' said Iestyn, straining his eyes.

Ianto, with the spy-glass, said, 'The lugger's putting about and leaving the line.'

Even with the naked eye they could see the distance between the lugger and the cutter lessen quickly as the two vessels approached one another. Then there was a puff of smoke from the lugger, followed by another and another, and the cutter was seen to lurch drunkenly with her main mast toppling.

'Diawl y manufferni,' Ianto said, 'White ensigns be buggered!'

'Now we know what we've got to beat,' Iestyn said. 'Just as
if we didn't know in the first place.'

(7)

All day they beat up into the wind and Preedy was at the
wheel as the others jumped to do old Iestyn's bidding,
tightening ropes or rigging here and slacking off a little there.
Close to Preedy he stood and said, 'Watch for that little
quiver until your eyes go crossed. Never mind about the
froggies. Every time you take your eyes off that sail we'll lose
a length or more. And we don't tack till they do.'

Preedy thought of the great ships coming up on them and
remembered the vast bulk of the Boadicea towering above
them at Buckler's Hard. From what Ianto Pugh had said
these could be even bigger. They could run the Dancing
Dervish down without knowing they had hit her. No need to
fire a shot. 'Twould be God help them all and especially God
help Beth. In spite of the cold the sweat rolled down his
forehead and he held his eyes firmly to the little quiver in the
mainsail where the gaff came down to the mast. And all the
time the Dancing Dervish ploughed into the steadily mount-
ing seas as the east wind blew stronger and his arms ached as
he held the wheel to keep her just into the wind.

'Let it blow,' said Iestyn, 'and the stronger the better.' His
eyes were everywhere. And then, at last, watching the
French squadron through his spy-glass, he called Ianto to
him and said, 'Take a look.'

'They're backing their topsails,' Ianto said.

'That's it then. Get ready to go about.'

Iestyn moved to the wheel and said, 'Leave her to me now,
my boy. You've done well.'

At last Preedy was able to look back and was frightened to
see how much closer the Frenchmen were, and to see the
great black-sided bulk of them towering out of the water as
they made light of the waves. Slowly they seemed to be
heading up into the wind, and then Iestyn spun the wheel.
Momentarily the Dancing Dervish stood with her bows into

the wind and then, with just one shout from the old seaman, the boom swung over, and sails were re-set as they drove into the wind on another tack. Preedy watched the French squadron and could see what a slow and clumsy manoeuvre it was for them to change course. And, as the Dancing Dervish sped away, he could see how the Frenchmen were still far in their lee and he felt a new hope.

So the day wore on as they beat up the Bristol Channel and, at every tack, the French were that much closer. As they came up off Lundy they encountered two ketches and a smack smaller than the Dancing Dervish. Unsuspecting, they held course and were sunk comprehensively by the ships flying their white ensigns. Late afternoon it was. And then, a brief exchange of signals between the French vessels and they hove-to. Watching through his spy-glass Iestyn saw that they had dropped anchor.

'What d'you think, Ianto?' he said.

'The same as you, bach.'

'Waiting for the tide so that they can go up with the flood?'

'Diawl, yes. What else whatever?'

'So how long does that give us?'

'Another four hours.'

Daniel had come up to join them and listened as they weighed up the situation.

'How would it be after dark,' he said, 'if we made a run for it with the wind?'

'No good at all,' said Iestyn.

'But the froggies would be beating up for Bristol and we'd be heading for home with the wind behind us.'

'And suppose they find this wind too much for 'em the same as happened at Bantry Bay and they head for Cardigan like we've been told their plans are? Daniel, boy, they'd be on us like a starving dog at a piece of liver.'

'Well, can't we put in somewhere?'

'What, with the cargo we've got on board?'

'Damn it, Uncle Iestyn, we could dump that or pay duty on it. Anything. I'm thinking of young Beth as much as ourselves. Can't you imagine what they'd do to her?'

Uncle Iestyn put his hand on Daniel's shoulder. 'Daniel, boy,' he said kindly. 'I'm your father's brother. I won't let you down. We've got four hours start on the froggies from here. Let's see how we stand at first light and if there's any danger at all we'll run her in somewhere. From now on we can get some sleep in turn. And my betting is if this wind'll keep up they won't get anywhere near Bristol even on a flood tide.'

'Duw, duw,' Ianto said, 'dump our cargo? There's enough on board to buy your ship for you.' Then his brown eyes smiled and said, 'Diawl y manufferni. Mad you must be. What would you do for ballast? Duw, duw, bach. You don't think we can't outsail the froggies do you? Dump a beautiful cargo like that. Duw, duw!'

Preedy had said nothing, but it renewed his confidence to hear these experienced hard-bitten seamen talking. And through the gathering gloom they sailed on steadily, snatching some sleep in turn, and Beth busy in the galley, until the moon was on the water, and they felt the flood tide beneath them. Yet still the wind blew steady and, even with the tide on the flood, by daybreak they had not gone much beyond Combe Martin, and the hills of Exmoor were on their starboard bow. Astern, the enemy were off Ilfracombe sinking a few merchant vessels as they came on.

So the flight and pursuit of the previous day resumed until they were off Porlock. And then there was a puff of smoke followed by two more and the shots fell far short of their target.

Charlie Wigan, standing at the rail laughed aloud and shouted, 'Never touched me! Never touched me!'

Ianto had the spy-glass and said to Iestyn, 'Duw, duw, bach. We've done it. They're wearing.'

Let me see. Ianto handed over the spy-glass. Quite clearly the French ships were turning their heads away from the wind.

'It's Cardigan Bay for them,' Iestyn said. 'And with this wind abaft their stern they won't be long about it.'

Even as he spoke, the menace with its great spread of canvass was receding in the distance. Nelson jumped down from the rail and went below.

'Best put about, Iestyn, is it?' Ianto said.

Preedy suddenly realised that for Ianto the worry was far from over. Cardigan was where his loved ones were. Then he thought of Beth and turned away so that the grown men should not see him cry, although his tears were only those of a great relief.

(8)

The rest of the voyage was as uneventful as that which had gone before had been memorable. Far from experiencing the gale which had threatened, the wind had eased, and the Dancing Dervish dropped anchor in the haven at Scalmey on Wednesday as the sun was setting in a red ball of fire in the west.

George Dawkes, who had worked on The Island most of his life, came down the track to meet them. He admired the Dancing Dervish, but was even keener to talk about the morning's happenings.

'By gaw,' he said, 'you've missed all the excitement. We had three great warships and a lugger sail up first thing this morning and they was a wonderful sight. Gaw boy, look here, don't talk. You've never saw ships like it.'

'Whose ships were they, George?' Daniel said.

'Why, ours boss. Gaw, boy, look here. I said we need never be afeart of no froggies nor nobody so long as we got ships like that to defend us.'

'Flying the white ensigns were they, George?'

'Why aye, of course they was.'

'And where'd'they go?'

'Last time I seen 'em they was up off the Bishops.'

'Heading for Cardigan Bay I expect.'

'I shouldn't wonder for all. But by gaw they was a wonderful sight.'

When they put Ianto Pugh ashore on the mainland on the Thursday afternoon they were greeted by a rumour that the

French had landed near Fishguard and that people were flee-
ing from their homes with what belongings they could carry.
Ianto, relieved to think that if it really was Fishguard, it was
not as bad as if it were Cardigan, decided not to wait or look
for a vessel but to make his way north on foot.

Iestyn said, 'Well, whatever's happening there'll be less
interest in what's going on down here, so we'll never have a
better chance to get shot of our lot.'

By the time they had shifted all their cargo the Dancing
Dervish was just about paid for, and then Jem Burlace and
Charlie Wigan went their separate ways.

(9)

As the days went by, the news came through how the
French had landed at Carreg Wastad, near Fishguard,
without meeting with any opposition, and how Castagnier
had sailed away with his squadron, leaving Tate and his
troups to get on with whatever job it was they had come to
do. They did indeed do much damage to farmsteads and
households in the surrounding area, but within a couple of
days had surrendered to Lord Cawdor and the Castlemartin
Yeomanry.

Nelson was brought ashore, took no more than three fights
to establish himself amongst The Island's colony of cats, and
founded a line of ginger cats which was to endure.

Beth, too, settled on The Island. Four years later she and
Preedy married and took over later when Daniel died.

Six children they had, five boys and a girl. Preedy still made
the occasional trip in the Dervish himself and always brought
back something special for Beth, especially on the occasions
when the children had been born. But, round about the time
of the end of the war, both he and Beth developed an interest
in fine china and porcelain, and it so happened that, also
round about that time, a pottery was set up making some
beautiful porcelain at Nantgarw in south Glamorgan. After
a while the business was merged for a time with a pottery at
Swansea. Beautiful the porcelain was, with a duck-egg finish

to some of it, and with lovely green borders and delightful floral patterns.

It also so happened that at that time Preedy made a number of calls at Swansea, and each time he brought Beth back some of the china. On one occasion he brought a whole dinner set, and on another a beautiful tea service. And he brought several individual pieces of distinction until Beth had to tell him to stop.

They were happy, untroubled days for them, with their young family growing up in the care-free home life of The Island. There was little indication of the hard times to come.

Chapter 7

The Nineteenth Century

(1)

Harder it was for Preedy Griffiths in middle age to learn so much of poverty and the struggle to live, because he had been brought up, and so many of his ideas had been fashioned, in an age of affluence. By the time he was old enough to be conscious of what was involved in acquiring the material things of life, the war with France had started and corn and stock and produce were selling well. But he was old enough to remember the time when old Uncle Iestyn had warned his father what would happen when he first began to talk of the possibility of buying a big boat. Now the war was over and the hard times had returned with a vengeance. Old Iestyn's words had long since come true.

It was with the potato famine in Ireland, a couple of years after the war, that the poverty began to make itself felt, with Irish peasants turning up begging for food and work. On The Island they suddenly realised that there was no demand for their corn, and land which had been ploughed was not even planted.

Then, in the middle of their troubles, because troubles always seemed to have a habit of coming all at the same time, old Daniel, with two men and a boy, was drowned when the Dancing Dervish foundered on the Wolves Teeth.

If there was any comfort to be had, it was in the knowledge that the old man had not lived to see his dreams in ruins, and the awful poverty which was even now upon the country people. The old Dervish, after nearly thirty years of wonderful service, would be sadly missed, but there could be no thought of replacing her.

The two farms in Cardiganshire, which had been inherited by the great Pryderi, had long since been sold. For a time Preedy thought about packing up and looking for a place on the mainland but, there, conditions, in many respects, were even worse. What had once been common land was being enclosed, and people were even moving to the higher ground to struggle for a living from the inhospitable hill country. The gentry, just by Acts of Parliament, seemed to be able to do whatever they liked.

Even out on The Island in early summer they made their presence felt. Of late they had taken to sailing round in their boats in great shooting parties. Only a few of them came at first, but now there were more of them at it. All day, some days, they would blaze away at the birds flying in terror from the ledges on the cliffs. Hundreds upon hundreds were killed outright, and as many again were wounded, to suffer, and eventually die in torment on the blood-stained water. And on the ledges, without food, their young were left to perish.

Since time out of mind the local people had gone down the cliffs for the sea-birds' eggs, and sometimes took the plump young to eat, but always the breeding birds had been left unmolested. And, when the first eggs had been taken, the birds would always lay again.

Then, one winter, the gentry came to shoot the pheasants and the partridges. Preedy knew how his Gramfer Owen had husbanded them, and what good sport there had always been, but now these knickerbockered louts blazed away at hens and cocks alike and, when there was nothing left to shoot, went away cheerful.

Like many other young country people, Daniel, Preedy and Beth's firstborn, had already despaired and left to seek his fortune in Canada. There was nothing to keep them at home. Rhiannon, who came next, loved The Island, but her younger brothers were far from content with their lot.

(2)

'There's not much to gain by grumbling,' Rhiannon said.
'I suppose not,' said Iestyn, 'but what be the point in it all?'
For a whole week he had been repairing the walls of the fields where cattle had been rubbing and gaps had appeared as the stones had fallen.

'There be no profit in grumblin', but there be no profit in nothin' else neither. Ever since the war finished things been gettin' worse. 'Tisn't worth puttin' the plough into a field no longer. When owld Napolean and the Frenchies had to be fought there was good prices to be had for everythin'.'

'Yes, but they were terrible times for everybody else with small children starving. What I'm afraid is that things are going to get far worse again before they get better.'

'If I thought 'twas gwain to get any worse I'd pack my bag tomorrow and over the ocean like Danny and the rest on 'em. The land have been took from people and what is there left for 'em? They can't graze their animals and they can't collect wood nor dig peat for firin'. They can't even cut a bit of rush for to thatch a roof.'

'I know all that. But what could Father and Mother do without us? Especially you two boys.'

Iestyn sighed. 'I've thought about that too. I'm alus thinkin' about it. 'Tis th'only reason I've stuck it so long. But what's here for you? You been schooled and been learnt music and sewin'. You could better yourself easy.'

'I know, I know!'

'And fair play to Father he alus says we must make out the best we can for ourselves. He can see what's happenin' as well as anybody.'

(3)

Cheerful though all the family tried to be at suppertime, sadness lay heavy on them throughout the meal. And through the night Rhiannon lay sleepless, excited at the prospect of the ocean journey which lay ahead, but grieving at the thought of leaving her home and family and The Island she loved. It was only the thought that Iestyn and Owen would be travelling with her that had enabled her to come to such a decision.

Eventually she rose and, barefooted, went to the window to gaze on The Island bathed in moonlight. No sound was there of any shearwaters. As dawn was breaking she dressed and, going downstairs quietly, went out into the sharp

morning air to leave her footprints in the dewy pasture.
Before she had reached the cliff-tops, larks were overhead
pouring out a cascade of song. Rabbits hopped away as she
walked, puffins, all curiosity, gathered in little groups, and,
way below them, two seals floated upright, heads turned
towards the cliff-top. The only sounds were of the bird calls,
and the sea breaking gently against the cliffs, and she knew
a terrible longing.

When she returned to the house Beth was already astir and
busy in the kitchen. Rhiannon knew her mother had been
weeping, yet, because of her own sorrow, could not trust
herself to comfort her.

She loved her parents and loved The Island. She was
dreading the parting.

(4)

'Of course, I don't remember my great great grandfather,'
said Rhiannon. 'The great Pryderi he's known as in the
family. He died years before I was born. But my father always
said he was a marvellous farmer. He had a wonderful eye for
stock and transformed The Island with walled-in fields,
improved the buildings and the house and grew wonderful
crops of corn. 'Tis a beautiful place is The Island.'

Her companion smiled at her. 'Then why,' said he, 'are
you sailing away from it?'

They were leaning on the rail of the great schooner, two
days out of port and Canada bound. They had met within an
hour or two of going aboard and had been immediately
drawn to each other. On her wrist she wore a bronze
bracelet.

'What is there to live for?' she said. 'Maybe I wouldn't have
emigrated on my own. But once my brothers made up their
minds to go I decided to go, too. Even Father has said the
good years are over.'

'Good years!'

'Well, they were good for the farmers.'

'They weren't much good for anyone else.'

'No, I know. But now there's nothing for anybody.'

'You've talked a good bit about the great Pryderi since we came aboard.'

'Well, in a way he represented The Island and all it stands for. He made it what it is. Now times are changing and the hard life is too much. Swimming horses to the mainland and taking cattle one at a time in the boat. No price on the corn or anything else. My brothers just became fed up at working to no purpose and without any hope for the future.'

'That's the same with all of us.'

'And my brothers never loved The Island like I do. I must have inherited it from my great great grandfather.'

'He must have loved it to do all the work he did.'

'Ah, but apart from that, his life was one long fairy-tale. It was from him this bracelet came down to me.'

She held out her wrist and the young man looked at it admiringly.

'My father said it came to Pryderi from his great grandmother, old Rhiannon, whose husband built up the family fortune. After that it was easy. A case of money makes money, until they lost just about everything in the South Sea Bubble. But the old man didn't seem to mind. He'd never been the least bit interested in the shipping and the dealing. As long as he had The Island and his princess as he called her.'

'His princess?'

'Yes. I told you his life had been a fairy-tale. He heard stories from his great grandmother when he was a small boy and just dreamed of The Island. He landed there when his father's ketch was wrecked and found this girl living there. She was a lot older than he was and had already had a child before she married. But he took to the child and they had four children of their own and were devoted to each other. They were married for more than fifty years, she nursed him through his last short illness, the only one he'd ever had, and within twenty-four hours had died herself of a broken heart.'

'Nice way to go. What plans do you have for yourself when you get to Canada?'

'None at all. My eldest brother is already there and it was he was so enthusiastic for us to go out. So my two brothers said let's give it a try, and here we are.'

'You have three brothers?'

'No, five altogether. Two more, younger again. But they're still working with Father. For the time being anyway.'

'Have you any sisters?'

'No. I'm the only girl. So I was the pet and they sent me to the mainland to school and to learn music and sewing. Quite the lady.'

'Won't they grieve at your leaving them?'

Tears came to the girl's eyes.

'Yes. But I expect I'll be going back. I couldn't bear to hurt them. And they know I love The Island. Funny really. The boys always wanted to be off but had to stay home to work. I always loved it and I was the one who was packed off to school.'

'Perhaps you wouldn't have loved it so much if you'd had to be stuck there all the time.'

Low above the water a group of shearwaters swept across their path. The girl had no difficulty in identifying them and telling her companion of their ways, where they nested, how they called on dark nights, and of how they were easy prey for the great-black-backed gulls to tear apart and devour. She told him of the birds of the ledges and of the puffins. Especially the puffins. From as early in her life as she could remember the puffins had been her favourites.

'You make it sound like Utopia.'

'Utopia? Where's that?'

'Utopia is an imaginary island in literature, created by Sir Thomas More, where everything is perfect.'

'Oh, no. It's not always been perfect. You must get my brothers to tell you the awful stories they have made up about the skeleton.'

'What skeleton?'

'The one that was dug up in the paddock near the house years ago when all the great work was going on with the field walls and improving the house and buildings. The skull had a bullet hole right between the eyes. A hideous thing. And the boys would put a candle in it at night and frighten the lives out of people who hadn't been to The Island before. In the end Father got so cross with them he threw it in the sea.'

'What's one poor skeleton on a place where people must have lived for God knows how many years?'

'Oh, there were dozens of skeletons at one time Father said. All in one great burial mound. When he was young he said the boys used to play bowls with the skulls. I can remember seeing one when I was small, but I haven't seen any this long time now.'

(5)

It was thus in talk of The Island that they passed the time on their voyage and, when she would prompt him, Julian Ray would tell her of his own life, his studies at Oxford and his dreams for the future. And then, on the day when they sighted land, he said,

'It is very impertinent of me, but I don't think you are wise to wear that beautiful bracelet on your wrist.'

'Don't you like it?'

'Its beauty is only surpassed by that of its wearer. But, apart from being a family heirloom, you will probably find that it is worth far more than you realise. I have had some small acquaintance with these things. There are others who might know as much, and both you and the bracelet could be at some risk.'

'All right. I'll take it off tonight and keep it safe.'

'That is a comfort. And you promise to write to me when you have settled?'

'I promise.'

(6)

Rhiannon's homecoming was far from being the joyful experience she would have envisaged when she set sail.

Not only had word come that her mother had died. There was a great emptiness in her heart which had been there ever since her beloved Julian had coughed himself to a pain-racked death. The years of self-denial whilst he studied had taken their inevitable toll. As soon as they had landed in Canada and he had found a job he had asked Rhiannon to marry him. Such a gentle nature he was, and their little Bethan had adored him. Now something of her childish grief seemed to have been forgotten in the excitement of coming back to The Island of which her mother had told her so much.

Preedy had sent the fare for Rhiannon to come home. She did not regret her decision to leave in the first place, but now she knew she would be happy to devote the rest of her life to her family. And The Island was in her blood.

Nearly ten years it was since she had gone away, and they were years which had taken their toll. Her father had aged terribly, but George and Jack had grown into fine young men.

It was in the house she saw the greatest difference. Since Beth had died there had been precious little cleaning done. And, hard though times were, she could not accept that they must needs have butter-milk and potatoes boiled in their skins to eat every day.

Bessie Dawkes was doing her best, but there was no firm hand to guide her. All day she shuffled about with her clogs clattering, but often with little purpose or direction in what she was doing. Far from resenting a new mistress, she welcomed someone to take a responsibility for which she was not by nature fitted.

There were plenty of rabbits to be had, and two hams which had never been touched hanging from the kitchen beam. Since Beth died nothing had been done in the garden, so Rhiannon had one of the farm boys and set him to work. In all her life on The Island she had never known them to be without vegetables. Poverty everywhere there may be, but there was no point in losing heart. That was not the pioneering spirit that had taken three of her brothers to Canada.

She was proud of the effort they were making out there in that land beyond the seas. Even so, she was disappointed when George and Jack decided to join them. Bethan, too, was sad because they had made a great fuss of her ever since she had arrived. Fair-haired and blue-eyed, like her grand-mother and namesake, she was about the fields with them all day long, sometimes carrying food to them, learning how to catch rabbits, and getting to know the different sea-birds when they came in the springtime.

It was at the time of the riots, when 'Rebecca' was terror-ising the countryside by night, that the boys eventually sailed to join their older brothers. Added to the sadness of parting was Rhiannon's worry about replacing them. Whoever they had would have to be paid and, however miserable a pittance it would be, it would still have to be found from somewhere.

Smashing the toll gates the riots were all about, so it was said, because of the charges for passing through with a load of lime or coal. But that was only the match which had touched off the powder keg which had been waiting for a long time for somebody to light it. The despair of the poverty, the workhouses, the poor law, tithes, taxes, high rents, the severity of transportation, and all the rest of the burden which the rural poor seemed to have to carry unaid-ed. With all their problems on The Island, Rhiannon, even so, was thankful they were away from all of that.

'God,' said Rhiannon, 'in the words of the hymn, moves in a mysterious way his wonders to perform.'

It was only a week after George and Jack had sailed that there came, in one of the fishermen's boats, a young man asking for Mr Preedy Griffiths. Of medium height, but broad of shoulder, he had a strong face which, every now and again, would suddenly light with an engaging smile. His hair was brown and his eyes were brown, but his complexion was not as dark as his grandfather's had been. And yet Preedy knew the features.

'My gramfer told me to come and see you,' the boy said. He was no more than a boy Preedy decided. Probably not yet twenty.

'And who is your gramfer?' he asked, 'And don't tell me. It wouldn't be Ianto Pugh would it?'

The boy laughed, 'He said you'd remember. From the smuggling run.'

Preedy gripped his hand, 'What's your name?' he asked.

'Evan. Evan Pugh.'

'Aye, smuggling!' Preedy said. 'That wasn't the half of it. But what brings you here?'

'I'm in trouble.'

'What sort of trouble?'

'Rebecca.'

'Oh, aye. Show me what they're bred from and I'll tell thee what to expect. Don't tell me your gramfer's involved in that as well.'

'Yes indeed.'

'And how old is he now?'

'Over eighty.'

Preedy laughed, 'I can hear him now—diawl y manufferni—mad you must be. You don't think we can't outsail the froggies do you? Dump a beautiful cargo like that. Duw, duw!'

'I'm glad you remember. Gramfer said you'd know about the chapel as well.'

'The chapel?'

'Well yes indeed. Our minister is preaching strong for Rebecca against the parsons and the tithes as well as the toll gates.'

'Which is your chapel then?'

'Well, duw, duw. It's the one the great Pryderi as they called him built. Gramfer used to put in here in one of the smacks when he first went to sea as a boy and the old gentleman used to talk to him a lot about the folks up there and his boyhood and all that.'

'Aye, well if your man is preaching against the parsons that would have suited old Pryderi no doubt.'

'Yes, indeed. Gramfer always used to say Pryderi was strong for the chapel and didn't mind the papists. Was big friends with one when he was young. But he couldn't abide the new religion the old English was trying to force on people. No use for parsons. Gramfer said the old gentleman said to him one day, ''They don't know what they believe

theirselves,'' he said. He said, ''They're like a lot of farts in a
colander and don't know which hole to come out of.'' '

They both roared laughing and Preedy said, 'Aye that's a
real old saying round here for all. And you reckon you're in as
much trouble now as when the froggies chased us that time?'

'It's as bad as that now, Mr Griffiths. If they do catch me
it'll be the hulks and Botany Bay or Van Dieman's Land for
sure.'

'So what d'you want me to do?'

'Gramfer thought you might be willin' to hide me till the
noise dies down a bit.'

'No need to hide over here, my boy. Would you like a job?'

'D'you mean that?'

'Why aye. How not? What can you do?'

'Anything you like on the land or with animals.'

'Can you handle a boat?'

The sudden smile was there, 'What? And me old Ianto's
grandson? I did spend hours in the boat with him fom the
time I could walk.'

(7)

For the two years before Preedy died, in the spring of 1849,
he had been a sick man, and Rhiannon had already taken
over responsibility outside as well as in the house. Evan had
remained on The Island and became her right hand man.
That summer he and Bethan were married. Rhiannon was
forty-six at the time.

Times were still bad, but there was talk of the railway
extending further into South Wales and she believed that,
with new markets thus becoming more accessible, the future
could hold out more hope. It was then that she crossed to the
mainland to see the Agent to the Estate. The existing lease
was to the end of her life. The Agent had little interest in The
Island and, although he pointed out that the system was falling into disuse, agreed to a new lease for two lives, those of
Rhiannon herself and of her daughter, Bethan Pugh. To the
Agent's surprise this rather determined lady, who seemed to
know exactly what she wanted, also insisted that the

agreement should include the game rights as well as the rabbits.

Even before the railway came as far as Carmarthen, times had begun to improve. Two itinerent Irishmen had turned up after the more recent potato famine in that unhappy land, and Rhiannon, with a tenderness engendered by what she had herself known of poverty, had found work for them to do. When they had made good the walling in all the fields Evan set them to work topping the boundary walls with heather to stop the rabbits jumping on top of them. As far as possible they would try to confine the rabbits to the rough land between the boundary walls and the cliffs.

So the sheep could be contained, and corn was grown again. Good corn it was, too, growing as high as a man's head, and much of it was sold for seed. Crossing cattle to the mainland was, as always, a challenge in the open boats, but as long as prices held good it was worth it.

Evan and Bethan had been married for ten years before Rhiannon became a grandmother. Two girls there had been to start, but both had died at birth. Then Owen arrived, lusty and powerful of lung, and, after another girl who died, came Preedy.

Rhiannon, prosperous, was well content. But there was one constant source of annoyance, which was why she had been so insistent on having all the shooting rights. Every summer one or more boatloads would come with parties for the senseless shooting of sea-birds, and now it had become even worse, for a steamer with a bigger party started to come. Then came those in search of the birds's wings for the latest craze for decorations for ladies' hats.

True, the fishermen would put nets below the cliffs to catch the puffins as they fluttered down to the sea to use them for bait in their lobster pots. Rhiannon did not mind this, nor did she mind the taking of the sea-birds' eggs from the ledges. Where it was for man's benefit, and could be properly managed, she believed it was as it should be. In the Bible at the beginning of creation it said that God gave man dominion over the fish of the sea, the fowl of the air, over the cattle and over all the earth and over every creeping thing that creepeth upon the earth. But she was angered by wanton destruction.

Over all the years the sea-birds' eggs and some of the young had been taken—and she knew all the stories from way back in time—there had been no diminution in their numbers. Not even when they used to take the puffins for their feathers, or for the papists to eat their flesh instead of fish in Lent. But now, gaps were appearing on the ledges in early summer, where previously the birds had bred. Sooner or later it would deprive the local poor people of what for generation beyond number had been part of their living.

Even worse than the indifference of the gunmen in leaving wounded birds to die on the water, and their young to die starving on the ledges, was the cold-blooded cruelty of the wing collectors who would cut off the wings, and then throw the birds into the sea, where they would struggle with feet and head until a lingering death could come to their relief.

Revolted almost beyond words, Rhiannon vowed to do whatever she could to goad authority into action. Parsons, preachers, landlords, magistrates all seemed to be indifferent. Then she read of a Member of Parliament for Yorkshire, a Mr Christopher Sykes, who was trying to put a stop to similar practices in his own area. So, heartened at last, Rhiannon sat down and, in her best handwriting, wrote to Mr Sykes and told him of all the things she had herself seen, of the damage being done, and what it meant to the poorer people of the coastal areas. In time Mr Sykes wrote back to her and, in a charming letter, asked her to keep him supplied with any information which she thought would be useful to him in his campaign.

Encouraged by this, Rhiannon wrote a letter to *The Times*, denouncing the fashion of decorating ladies' hats with birds' wings, and in which she said, 'far from wearing such adornments with pride they should hang their heads in shame in the knowledge that they bear the brand of the murderer upon their brow.'

Writing, as she did, from the first-hand experience which she was able to quote, her letter caused considerable interest, and she received, amongst others, a letter from Mr Sykes encouraging her and urging her to keep up the pressure.

Rhiannon felt a glow of pride when Mr Sykes, with support from many influential quarters, succeeded in getting the Sea Birds Preservation Act through Parliament in the summer of 1869. She cared not in the least that the Act still permitted the taking of the sea-birds' eggs.

(8)

Pleased though Rhiannon was at the success of the campaign, it was the farming achievement which gave her the real satisfaction. The railway had indeed opened up vast new markets in the valleys of industrialised Glamorgan and beyond. There seemed to be a ready demand at steady prices for everything they could produce.

For all their island remoteness there was modern machinery, too. The corn ricks were still built alongside the barn, but the old-fashioned hand-flails, for beating out the corn on the stone floor, had long since been replaced by a threshing machine in the barn, which was driven by a horse-course outside. All day long in the threshing season the horses walked round the capstan on the circular course, and the power was used to drive the chaff-cutter as well, chopping up the long straw and the furze for the horses.

All this arable land, of course, as well as the grassland, needed lime, and anthracite was brought in to keep the lime-kiln busy burning the limestone. A busy time it was when the smacks landed the coal on the beach and, between tides, the horses and carts plied to and fro, up and down the steep track.

Then there were the fourteen milking cows which kept the milk-maids and the dairy-maids occupied from morning till night. A hundredweight of butter was made every week all through the spring and summer, and there were the calves and the pigs to be fed on the skim milk.

Five men on the land there were. In the summer they were out and about before five o'clock in the morning going round the sheep, for by day the sheep were difficult to find, sheltering in the shade of the rocks and cliffs. Then, in the evenings, the men had to go round them again. And the fat cattle, too, did well on the rich summer grazing.

Both the Irish boys were good with horses and each year a few colts would be broken in and sold to the mainland.

For several weeks in the winter the rabbit catchers came, and Rhiannon insisted that they used only ferrets and dogs and no traps, which meant that there were not now too many rabbits to damage the corn crops and the grass which could be put to better purpose. But the pheasants and partridges were reintroduced, and the wild-duck and the woodcock still came in winter, so that there was plenty of good shooting for the boys when they came to handle a gun.

From an early age Rhiannon had taught the boys to read and write and had encouraged them to go on reading. And, in the tradition which had come down to them from at least as far back as the great Pryderi, she saw to it that the Bible was not neglected, and the custom was continued of morning prayers every day and a service on Sunday.

How much this influenced the servants she was not sure, for two of the girls in successive years came crying to her to say they were with child. And in each case the culprit was a lad who had come over with the rabbit catcher. Rhiannon knew the story of her own ancestor of long, long ago. And she recognised the temptations, too, when the men and girls all slept in the lofts above the stables. In many cases on the mainland, she knew, conditions were infinitely worse. And at least the girls were not turned out to fend for themselves.

With all this activity they no longer relied on their own two boats on The Island, but maintained another boat on the mainland which was worked by the Rafferty family. Rhiannon paid them a small wage and so much for every trip. At other times they had the boat for their own use.

(9)

The first indication that the good days were at an end came with the weather. It began with a sodden, rain-ruined harvest, which was followed by another and yet another. For three years in succession they gathered but little corn and yet, what little they did harvest, far from making the high prices to have been exepected in a time of scarcity, sold for poorer prices than they had received for years, because the country had plenty of corn which had been imported from the prairies of the Middle West.

It was then that Rhiannon died, suddenly and peacefully, as if, in her seventy-eighth year, everything had become too much for her.

When the Rafferty boys came with the coffin the sky looked as if a storm could be blowing up. So they took Rhiannon over and had her funeral that same day. The local fishermen and the poor people who paid their last respects knew they had lost a good friend. It was late when they got back to The Island. That night there was a great autumn storm and they saw no one for a fortnight.

Without Rhiannon's guiding hand, Evan and Bethan talked far into the nights, as the wind howled about them, as to what they should do. Certainly there was no point in all the work and expense of growing corn if they were unable to sell it. And much the same thing seemed to be starting to happen with everything else. There was talk now of meat and butter being brought from the colonies in refrigerated ships. It was all more than they could cope with, especially since workers in industry were earning more money, so that farm-workers were asking for higher wages as well.

'There's only one thing to do,' Evan said, 'keep less hired help, do the best we can, and I'll start catchin' lobsters and rabbits myself. And we'll swarm the rabbits as well.'

So it was that Owen joined his father in the boat, and young Preedy, not yet twenty, went off to be a soldier. He saw much of the world whilst life remained to him, and his letters were regular, if not frequent, but they were never to see him again

for he was killed at Khartoum, at the same time as General
Gordon, three years later.

Nobody was there now to repair the field walls and, once
the gaps appeared, it was not long before the sheep and cattle
made them bigger, and soon they had the run of The Island
from one end to the other. Nor did they make any butter, but
Bethan just kept a couple of cows for the house.

'May as well be a idle fool as a busy fool,' she said.

Evan and Owen did well enough on the lobsters and the
rabbits, and they killed seals in the autumn, and shot them
sometimes in the water. The pelts were useful and some sold
for good money.

Taller than his father Owen was, and broad of shoulder,
with his mother's colouring, fair haired and blue-eyed. More
than one of the girls looked his way when he and his father
used to cross to the mainland to cut withes for making their
lobster pots, but Owen had little interest for a long time. Not
until Will Rafferty was drowned only a few years after he
married.

A trim cottage he had and a good garden, but Dolly, his
young widow, was just a bit helpless. And Will had done
many kindnesses for Owen and his father, so it was only
natural that Owen should help where help seemed to be
needed. Two years running he dug and planted her garden
for her, and he white-limed the cottage as well. Then it came
on to blow one night, and he was unable to get back to The
Island, so he slept the night with Dolly and after that the
proper thing to do was to marry her.

So Owen lived on the mainland now, and went to The
Island most days when the weather answered, and he did a
bit with a few sheep and cattle when it was necessary, and he
and his father still worked their lobster pots together. Until
one day late in the decade which was to become known as the
Hungry Nineties, when Evan was out in the boat on his own,
and the wind freshening suddenly, the Wolves Teeth claimed
another victim.

It was not long before Bethan agreed that the sensible thing
to do was to move over to live with Owen and Dolly.

In the fullness of time they had one son, and they named him Preedy, after Owen's brother who had been killed 'out foreign'.

Chapter 8

The Twentieth Century

(1)

The ball fire in the fisherman's cottage was burning with a cheerful blue flame where the poker had been used to make two holes in the culm which had been stummed down all night. On the hob the big black kettle steamed ready for use, and the lurcher stretched out on the mat after a few hard days' work on The Island, Nelson, the ginger cat, was curled up alongside him. Nelson had come as a kitten from The Island, where there had always seemed to be a Nelson amongst the colony of ginger cats. It had become almost a tradition.

The flame of the fire was mirrored a score of times in the polished oak of the table and chairs, and the dresser with its polished brass drawer handles. But even the classic beauty of the dresser was outdone by the array which it bore of Nantgarw and Swansea china.

Bent now, and slow in her movements, old Bethan Pugh still retained a lively interest in all that was going on. On this trip Owen had brought back more than five hundred rabbits.

As he sat eating his meal she plied him with questions.

'Well, if it goes on like this,' he said, 'I reckon we'll catch more than ten thousand this winter.'

'That's a powerful lot of rabbits for one season.'

'Well, the place is swarmin' there now.'

'Is it indeed?'

'Aye, 'tis. And 'tis sad to see everythin' gwain to rack and ruin out there. The roof of the stable is gone altogether now since the last storm and the windows and doors all broke and hangin' loose.'

'What about the land?'

'That bain't so bad yet for all. But the brambles and fern is startin' to spread.'

She poured boiling water into the big brown teapot and left the tea to brew.

'Ah, well,' she said, ''Tis like everythin' else. Everythin' is changing so fast. I can mind Queen Victoria comin' to the throne and now she's dead the same as any ordinary mortal. And look at the changes we've saw in her time. When Mother and her brothers went out to Canada it was in great schooners. And Mother came back in a schooner as well. Now 'tis nearly all steamers.'

'They're a lot quicker, Mother.'

'Maybe so. But I don't hold with it. It's not natural. So no good will come of it.'

Owen said nothing. It was not the sort of thing his mother would normally have said. Always she had been far-sighted and willing to move with the times. Of late, however, she had begun to say and do little things which were out of character.

By the time the birds returned in the springtime, and the lobster pots were again being set, it was clear that she was failing. Then, one day, she asked for her box. It had been under her bed for years without being opened. From it she took a piece of velvet which she unwrapped and then held up a bracelet of burnished bronze.

Owen had often been shown the bracelet when he was a boy. It was some years since he last remembered seeing it, but he had been told stories beyond number concerning its long history.

'You knows this bracelet,' said his mother. 'Whatever else have happened to it we knows it have been all the way to Canada and back. For Mother wore it when she was a girl. Don't you never sell it because it have been handed down for hunderds of years so they reckons. Mother said as 'twas gave by her great gramfer, the great Pryderi, to the girl he married who was livin' on The Island as a housekeeper. Her name was Beth, too. And Mother was called Rhiannon after the great Pryderi's great grandmother who was brought up on The Island. And she alus reckoned that the name and the bracelet had been in the family for hunderds of years afore that. They reckons nobody knows the true story of it altogether.'

Owen handled the bracelet carefully with his rough hands.

His mother seemed to be forgetting how many stories she had told him about the bracelet over the years.

'No,' he said, 'I shan't sell it.'

'And your wife won't sell it?'

'Nobody shall sell it.'

'That's right then. Keep it for young Preedy when he grows up. If you don't have no more children then maybe he'll marry and have a daughter he can give it to. And he can call her Rhiannon after Mother.'

Already Preedy was going in the boat with him absorbing all the lore of his father's calling. Owen doubted whether there would be any more children. And his own brother, so long his only boyhood playmate when they had been brought up together on The Island, had gone off to the army never to return.

As his mother had said, everything seemed to be changing. Apart from the puffins and the other sea-birds. They kept coming back year after year, the same as they had been doing since time began, but even they seemed to be getting fewer every year. So, whatever the Act to protect them was supposed to have done, it did not seem to be protecting them very much. Nobody took them in the nets now, nor shot them, nor took them for food, and still their numbers seemed to be declining. Only the ginger cats seemed to be increasing out there.

Maybe his mother had been right after all. Nothing made sense any more.

(2)

Preedy had been going in the boat with his father before he had started school, and he had few real memories either of his mother or his grandmother. Both of them, he knew, had died within a short time of each other. So there was only his father and himself now and they were inseparable.

Owen had been taught by his grandmother, Rhiannon, to read and write, and now he taught and encouraged young Preedy. But, at week-ends, at holiday time, and on as many days as possible in the long summer evenings, he would be away with his father in the boat, working the lobster pots or roaming The Island in search of rabbits.

He loved The Island and never wearied of listening to his father's stories of what life there had been like. His father had been born there.

His father's mother, old gran Bethan, had been born in Canada and brought home to The Island as a small girl. Her father and mother had met on board the ship going out and had married out there. But her father had died young of consumption, brought on, so it was said, by his years of studying at Oxford when he often had scarcely enough money to buy food.

'Rhiannon,' said Owen, 'was the name of the girl who went out to Canada. That was my mother's mother. And her five brothers all went out as well at different times. But we haven't heard tell of them for years now. I can mind old Rhiannon well. Brought my mother back as a little girl from Canada and ran the farm after her father died. Loved the old place. Taught us boys to read and write. Wonderful woman she was and she could handle the boat as good as a man. My father married in, but by the time Rhiannon died farmin' was gone very bad. We hung on for a spell but we was makin' more on the rabbits and lobsters. Then I met your mother when we came out to the mainland to cut withes for lobster pots. So there 'twas. Father was drowned, my brother had been killed in the army and your gran came to live with your mother and me.'

Long before this, he said, the farming on The Island had decayed. Not for some years had any corn been grown, and the only butter being made had been for their own use. Great gaps were in the walls and the sheep had very nearly had the run of The Island from one end to the other. And, although a few horses had been kept for the odd jobs, no longer had colts been bred and broken in.

(3)

With his own involvement in the boat it was only natural that Preedy should always be asking more questions, and listening even more avidly to stories about the wild-life, than about the farming. And so, at an early age, he had built up in his mind a complete picture of how the men stretched nets under the cliffs where the puffins fluttered down to the sea, to be caught and used as marvellous bait for the lobster pots.

Eventually the Act had been passed which made it an offence to do this, but the puffins were still declining in number.

It was not safe now to put out a net to catch the puffins, for some busybody would see it and report it. But at night by lamplight it was not difficult to collect a bagful of shear-waters as they emerged from their nests and fluttered help-lessly about The Island trying to become airborne, and they made good bait too.

Preedy had already become expert in setting the pots round the cliffs and had come to know the best places where, deep down in the dark waters, the lobsters and crayfish could be caught.

'Always have a crayfish if you can,' said his father. 'A lobster's all right but sometimes they tends to be a bit watery. But a crayfish is always meat right through. And when it comes to cookin' 'em, no matter what size they be, twenty minutes in boilin' water and no more.'

The seals, however, seemed to be increasing. Now that there was no longer anybody living on The Island not many seals were being killed and there was even talk of protecting them.

In the autumn, said his father, before the rabbit seasons really started, they used to spend several days years ago killing seals. Clubs they used, killing the seals by hitting them on the nose, and many were the uses to which the skins had been put including warm coats for the men in winter. The fat from the seals had been rendered down and used for greasing the cart axles and farm machinery. Years ago, it was said, the oil had been used for lighting and even for cooking, and at one time there had been stories of people salting down the seal meat and eating it like pork.

Later in the winter, if they were not on the rabbits, they would be making lobster pots ready for the summer.

'From young withes they was made,' said Preedy's father, 'the same as we does now. But there was never no trees of any kind on The Island because of the salt wind burnin' everythin' off. So we had to come out to the mainland to cut 'em. And that's how I met your mother.'

And at mention of his wife he would go quiet for a while. Life had not been kind to him. But he had his boy, and his cottage, and his boat. And the old bronze bracelet which his mother had always treasured, as well as the old oak dresser and table and chairs, and china which, so some folks said was beyond price. He had his books, too. He treasured his books.

(4)

Preedy had few friends outside of school and took little part in games. The life he had was all he needed, and occasionally even this provided its extra excitement such as the time, when he was still quite young, when he worked a trip on one of the Breton langoustiers.

For years these Breton ships, fishing for lobsters and crayfish, had anchored in the shelter of The Island and his father was friendly with some of the crews. It was a family friendship that went back to the time of the French wars. They, too, had once used puffins as bait for their pots, and still used shearwaters when Owen could get them some. And many a litre of red wine had he received in return for these and the rabbits he always gave them.

Preedy soon recognised these Bretons as kindred to his own people when, on a trip when one of their boats had put to sea one short of their normal crew of seven, one of them had met with an accident. Seriously short-handed, the Captain had asked Owen for help and he had let Preedy go with them.

It was a great adventure, sailing as far as the Hebrides and back down the west coast of Ireland to fish round the Blaskets.

Most of the crew spoke a little English and he soon picked up something of their own native tongue. The captain's son, Gaston, was the same age as himself and they became firm friends.

He learned much, too, of their fishing technique, being particularly interested in their casiers, a different type of lobster pot from those his father used, being of age-old design the crew said. They were round, with netted ends and an entry, behind part of which the bait was fastened.

From the Blaskets they sailed back to their native port of Camaret in Brittany. Then they did another trip south of Cassablanca as far as Oran in Algeria before returning, once more with a full crew, to The Island.

Before Preedy had sailed, his father had given him a fine old seaman's belt and a knife, so sharpened over the years, that it had become more like a stiletto.

'A fisherman needs a knife,' he said. 'I wish I had a shilling for every fish I've gutted and every rabbit I've paunched with him. And one day I'll tell thee a few stories about that owld knife as well.'

Preedy had much to tell his father when he came back. He had gone to sea as not much more than a boy at the beginning of the season. He returned a young man.

The trip had done much to widen his horizons and his outlook on life. He began now to turn to the books he read with a new interest.

Chapter 9

The Naturalists

(1)

More cautiously than ever before, the puffin moved from the darkness of the burrow out into the sunlight. Nowadays there always seemed to be danger. Yet, too late, he felt the thin wire round his neck, and, with wings beating furiously, he was pulled towards the creature and dropped into the smothering darkness of a sack where other puffins already lay tightly packed, one upon another.

Three more puffins were thrown in upon them before the puffin felt the sack moving. Crowded as they were some of the birds fought for space to breathe. Some were still and others trampled on them to stay near the top of the pile where the air was.

At last the puffin felt himself being taken from the sack and the creatures looked at him and made strange noises. Then he felt something being fastened on his leg and, with heart beating wildly, he was taken outside and cast into the air.

Rejoicing in his freedom he flew high across The Island and swooped down over the cliff for the sea. On the cliff-side brambles grew. And on one of the bushes a puffin fluttered helplessly, held by the thing on its leg which had caught in the brambles. Before nightfall the carcass had been stripped clean by a black-backed gull, and the puffin was afraid to return to the land.

Once back in the water and swimming freely the puffin began to feel safer. But the thing on his leg was irksome and he tried, without success, to tear it off with his beak. As the days passed he became more accustomed to it and, by the time he was well out to sea, he went for long periods without noticing it.

His greatest danger now seemed to be the dark patches on the water. Last winter he had swum into such a patch and found his feathers sticking together with black oil. Frantically he had spent days cleaning the oil off with his beak and then, for a long time, he had felt ill and scarcely had the strength to fly or look for food. During that time many other birds had died upon the water with their feathers covered with oil. He would be careful to watch for the dark patches on the water.

It was nearly spring again when one day, as he tried to fly, he felt a weight holding him back, and he was unable to rise from the water. Caught in the ring on his leg was a bunch of seaweed and, no matter how he tried, the puffin could not free himself.

Once, he had seen one of the great white gannets in a similar plight. Day after day it was in the sea, held down by the weight of the seaweed, and unable to rise and dive for fish. At last it had grown too weak to defend itself against the great black-backed gulls which had killed it. And now the puffin must face the same death.

The waves rolled over him and all he knew was a great noise and a blackness more lonely than any burrow he had ever explored on The Island.

(2)

The man, like the young chief who had come to The Island long ago, had hair on his face and down to his shoulders. His clothes, however, were different from those of that young chief, being of poorer quality and less tidy. He also wore steel-rimmed spectacles and a long woollen scarf, and on his feet there were sandals.

'Only ten more puffins to dissect', he said, 'and I'll have enough gen to finish my thesis.'

'You're lucky,' said the girl. 'I've only been able to ring two hundred puffins so far this season and the target is three hundred. I'm even down on last year's figure and I'm fifty short on the shearwaters as well.'

'What about the razorbills and guillemots?'

'Disastrous. There aren't any worth speaking of on the usual ledges so we're having to try to design a much longer rod with a net on it.'

'Nothing to do with the letters?'

'They don't help, of course.'

'Who the hell is she?'

'Some stupid old fool who doesn't believe in interfering with nature. Says she has had reports of the gulls stealing the eggs from the ledges whilst we've had the razorbills and guillemots up here to ring.'

'Interesting point for the gull thesis.'

'No help to me though.'

They were in what had once been the stable and which was now being used as a laboratory. Some dead puffins had been tipped from a sack onto a bench ready to be opened up for the contents of their stomachs to be analysed. Those which had not smothered in the sack were being ringed and weighed prior to being released by a group of three people who paid no heed to the conversation of the other two.

All five turned towards the door, however, as an older man came in waving a newspaper.

'News from the mainland, boys and girls,' he beamed. 'Another letter from our dear friend the nature lover declaring that, even when the gulls do not steal the eggs from the ledges, by the time we have ringed the birds and they have been released, the eggs have gone cold and will be addled.'

'She must be addled in the head,' said the scarf.

'And that bloody fisherman doesn't help.'

'What's the fool been doing now?'

'Not doing. Saying. Some little whippersnapper of a reporter got hold of him and quoted him as saying that there aren't half as many birds here now as when he was a boy.'

'Oh, for God's sake, not again! As if anybody of any intelligence would take any notice. No records to prove it. No scientific evidence. The summers were always hot and the grass was always green. Haven't you got anything more interesting than that to report?'

'Ha, ha, my boy. I was wondering when somebody would ask. Yes indeed. We're to have our own boat at last.'

'You mean we won't be dependent on that fool in his clapped-out tub any more? What a dimwit he is. He's got no more understanding of what's going on around him than the day he was born.'

'The locals are all the same. You should have had as much to do with 'em as I have.'

'What's the latest news of the bracelet?' the girl asked.

The older man roared laughing.

'Charles says he can't make it out. He's quite certain it must have been turned up on one of the digs over here, but the old fool keeps yammering on about it being given to him by his grandmother and such a crazy cock-and-bull yarn as you've never heard.'

'I wonder if he'd let us have it for ringing one of our more special specimens.'

As the laughter subsided a quiet young man said, 'Has it ever occurred to any of you that he might just know something about this place? His father was born here and he isn't exactly a fool.'

'Why don't you stick to chasing the butterflies little flower!'

Ignoring this the young man said, 'I've been in his cottage. He keeps it clean, he's surprisingly well-read, and when some of you smartie pants manage to run the new boat aground I'll make two guesses as to who'll have to sort you out again.'

'Oh, my goodness,' said the scarf, 'It isn't a lepidopterist we have in our midst after all. It's a prophet. A bloody prophet and a Jonah and a fifth columnist all rolled into one.'

(3)

Somewhere in middle age, Preedy, blue eyes smiling, sat on a log above high-water mark. His fair hair had kept its colour, and his seaman's cap was pushed back from the wide fore-head which topped a weather-beaten face. He wore a seaman's thick jersey and smoked a pipe with noonday satisfaction.

He chuckled as he said to the man sitting next to him, 'Drop dead, you'd think nobody'd ever had a boat or done anything on The Island before. Have you ever saw such a fandango in all your life!'

Below them on the beach, photographers and reporters were busy as The Islanders 'took delivery' of their new boat riding at anchor off-shore. A bottle of champagne was opened, there was a naming ceremony, the scarf looked studious, the older man did his best to look benign and the cameras clicked.

'What d'you think of her?' asked Preedy's companion.

Preedy took his pipe from his mouth and smiled. 'A lovely boat. As nice a boat as I ever saw round here. And she won't last the first winter.'

'You think not?'

'Why no! She don't draw enough water to go near the Dead Man's Race if the wind is anywhere but off the land.'

'She's all right today though.'

'Oh, aye, she's all right today. A hell of a good boat today.'

Of a morning not much more than a week later Preedy had just cleared the table and 'put his cottage to rights' for the day. It was a day when some little incident had set him thinking of the young wife who had died, along with their first-born child, and left him on his own. He had never wanted to remarry and he had no relations. Of those who had gone overseas nothing had been heard for many years.

He was just thinking of making a cup of tea, and wondering whether it would be fit to go out to his lobster pots, when his reverie was interrupted by a polite knock on the door. It was the young lepidopterist.

'Come in,' said Preedy, 'I'm just putting the kettle on.'

'I'm sorry to trouble you but . . .'

'It's no trouble. Always glad to see you, you know that.'

'I was wondering whether you'd seen anything of our people this morning?'

'Not a sign of 'em.'

'No sign of the boat?'

'Good God no. She won't come out in this weather.'

'Is it that bad then?'

'No, not like that. But that boat you've got would be arse over head in two minutes.'

The young man frowned. 'Oh, dear,' he said. 'It's terribly important for me to get back today.'

'Have a cup of tea first. And if there's no sign of 'em then I'll drop you over there when I goes out to the pots.'

'Would you mind?'

'Why no, not a bit. I've done it often enough before.'

'That was different. Before the great Island Enterprise was launched. But I don't mind telling you that I'll feel a lot safer with you than with some of those big-headed clowns over there.'

'What's the latest news there?'

The young man smiled. 'Rather serious I'd say. The most accommodating of our young ladies is in the pudding club as I believe you call it and they can't agree who is responsible.'

The fisherman roared laughing. 'Ah well. You'll have to start putting rings on them next to keep track of their movements.'

'Don't talk to me about their ringing. They're putting up even bigger traps now to drive the poor blighted migratory birds into them. Some sanctuary it's become.'

The fisherman filled his pipe and said, 'I know. When I was a lad going out there with Father you could collect a bucket of eggs on ledges where now you won't see a bird.'

'They reckon over there that it was all the taking of the eggs started the decline.'

'What do they know about it? The old timers only ever took one lot of eggs and then the birds laid again. You've saw what's happening with the gulls. They'll keep laying after their eggs have been took. Now nobody takes 'em and the gulls is getting the upper hand there. Stealing the other birds' eggs and killing the shearwaters and young puffins and the young birds off the ledges by the hundred.'

'Do you think the ringing has caused the decline in the number of birds?'

'Well it can't help 'em to increase can it? It's no benefit to the birds.'

'What do you reckon is the real cause?'

'Oil mostly. Ever since the coming of steam and oil. Bilge oil a lot of it. Oiling up the birds at sea and destroying the birds' natural food. Now when they comes to land to breed the gulls are tormenting 'em all day long. And when the gulls aren't tormenting 'em it's the ringers. The very ones who ought to be protecting 'em are the ones hindering 'em most. And they'll defend what they're doing till the last puffin is gone from there.'

As Preedy had predicted there was no sign of the new boat. Not until they rounded the headland and saw her holed up on the rocks near the Wolves Teeth. A scarf was being waved from the rocks.

'Ah well,' said Preedy, 'they won't come to much harm there for a few hours. What say I land you first, then send for the lifeboat? 'Twill make a better story for the papers than if I was to fetch 'em myself. Perhaps we'll give young Jim Sefton the tip as well.'

Epilogue

(1)

Preedy was old now. His blue eyes retained their brightness, but his hair was white and his step was slower.

His garden was still tidy and well kept, scarcely ever without vegetables and always with an abundance of flowers in season. But only rarely now did he put to sea, although he could not bring himself to part with his old boat. His had been the last boat to fish from the village.

'When I was a boy,' he would say, 'there used to be a dozen boats getting a good living.'

Since those days times had changed. What few lobsters and crayfish there were the skindivers took, and not for many years had it been possible to put down a net for clean fish. Protected now, the seals had increased to such numbers that they would tear a net to pieces in a matter of hours.

Perhaps once or twice in the course of a summer, when he was young, he would see a seal come up from under the water to take a swimming puffin in its strong jaws. Now it had become an every day occurrence and there were few puffins to be seen. The ledges, once thronged with razorbills and guillemots, were almost bare, and the gulls, which now filled the air in white clouds, were the only ones to be thriving.

At his age, what could there be left to him but his garden?

The letter had given life a new meaning.

Nothing at all did he know of relations. His grandmother, he knew, had been born in Canada, and her mother's brothers had all remained there. But not for many years had there been word of any of their families. And now this girl Rhiannon had written to him.

As she stepped from the hire car which had brought her from the station he felt a sudden excitement. Had he been told to look for his own grandmother, Bethan, as he remembered her from a picture taken when she was young, he might have been better prepared.

Rhiannon, who had not known what she would find, or what sort of reception to expect, was perhaps even more surprised to find herself with a strong arm round her shoulders and her first words were, 'I feel as if I'm coming home.'

Though she had asked the driver of the car to wait it was not long before she paid him off. Before the evening she had 'phoned for him to take her to the hotel, where she had booked, so that she could collect her luggage and pay for the room she would not now be needing.

Everything about the cottage and the old man's talk thrilled her. He was, she said, the living image of one of the brothers who had gone out to Canada all those years ago, and whose picture was still there in her home in a place of honour on the wall, and she was soon calling him Grandpa.

The brothers, she said, had all done well but only two of them had married. Apart from Preedy's own grandmother, Bethan, who had been born in Canada and brought back to The Island as a little girl, Rhiannon said that she herself was the only girl to have been born out there. Now somewhere in her twenties she had not yet married.

'Gee, Grandpa,' she said when he asked her why, 'I've got three or four fellahs asking me and I can't make up my mind between them. So I guess none of 'em can be the right one.'

He loved her sense of humour, and late each night they sat up talking about The Island and the family. A great researcher into the family history, she knew more about them than the old man, but there were still gaps here and there which he was able to fill in for her, as he told her all the folklore and stories way back to the earliest settlers.

About her own name she knew only that she had been christened after the girl who had gone out to Canada with the brothers and come back as a young widow.

'So who would she have been, Granpa?'

'That was my great grandmother. My grandmother's mother. She came back to The Island to her parents and took over when they died. My gramfer, Evan Pugh, married in as they say. Married Bethan as was born in Canada and brought back by her mother. Then times went very bad, so Father moved out here to the mainland and by the time I was born

Gramfer had been drowned and Father was just a fisherman the same as everybody else. His brother was killed out in India and now I'm the only one left.'

'Well where did the name Rhiannon come from? Would you know that?'

'Oh, that's a very old name. If you'll read the Mabinogion you'll see something about it there.'

'What's the Mabinogion then?'

'The Mabinogion? That's reckoned to be about the oldest Welsh writing there is. The name was originally Rigantona and she was selected by the king of the Otherworld who took on earthly form and changed places with an earthly king to mate with Rigantona and produce a wonder child called Pryderi. I don't think the poor soul was treated very well in the end, but that's where the name started and then changed over the years to Rhiannon. But you'll have to ask somebody who knows Welsh to explain about that.'

'Where did all this happen?'

'Oh, round these parts.'

'Why is it then that you can't speak any Welsh?'

'Our people have been here, mind, right from the beginning. But then the Celts came, then the Saxons after the Romans, and then the Normans settled a lot of Flemish weavers here. So what with one thing and another the language died out and we're a bit of a mixture altogether. But we belong here all right, never fear.'

Then he told her of the bracelet and how it had always been handed down. When he showed it to her she gazed at it in wonder for a long time before she could speak. Then she only said, 'Why, Grandpa, isn't it just beautiful!'

He thought for a while and, with a smile, said, 'So it'll be yours now won't it?'

'Mine, Grandpa?'

'Aye, yours. It have always been that it must be handed down in the family and I got nobody else to give it to.'

'But, Grandpa, I couldn't take this off you. I have all the money I shall ever want, but this must be priceless.'

'Ah, but that got nothing to do with it, maid. This isn't about money. It's about family. Flesh and blood. There's still some things as can't be bought with money.'

Again she looked at it for a long time, then shook her head in disbelief and said, 'Do you know anything of its history?'

'My great grandmother, Rhiannon, wore it when she went to Canada and brought it back with her. There's all sorts of other stories about Vikings and a Welsh princess and slave traders and I don't know what all. The old stories tell how it belonged to the first Rhiannon who was married to the young chief way back in the times of the early Celtic settlers. But it'll take a long time to tell you all those stories.'

'Gee, Grandpa,' Rhiannon said, 'all these stories ought to be written down.'

'Why no! They only concerns us in the family.'

'But all the stories about The Island! What about the folks over there now? Don't you think they'd like to know?'

'What? Them? They're only a heap of thunderin' gumps.'

'What's a gump then, Grandpa?'

'Well dullins, then. A heap of dullins.'

'So what's a dullin?'

Preedy took his pipe from his mouth and said, 'Well let's say as 'tis them as is too damn dull to know they're dull. What do they want to know about a bracelet as have been in our family since time out of mind like the owld writers used to say?'

He tapped out his pipe in the fireplace and said, 'And now it belongs to a Rhiannon once again.'

With tears in her eyes she slipped the bracelet onto her wrist.

(2)

Preedy had never wanted a television set, so they did not see the programme. But Jim Sefton of Fleet Street saw it and, from the days when he had been a junior reporter on the local paper, he remembered having seen the bracelet. Now he knew that he had a scoop as he drove through the night to be knocking on the cottage door early the next morning.

'It's true,' he said. 'They showed a bracelet which was a
twin to yours. It's been in a museum for hundreds of years
and the experts refused even to put a price on it. They reckon
that Celtic legend has it to be that originally there would have
been two and that they were worn by the ruler of a tribe and
his woman. But there's no known record of there ever having
been a second bracelet.'

Within twenty four hours the story was making the news
headlines. Being able to locate the bracelet would have been
more than sufficient compensation for the long drive he had
undertaken. To find Rhiannon there as the new inheritor was
the sort of story which in all his hard-bitten experience he
had never dreamed he would stumble upon.

Within days there were letters from museums, cultural
societies and, finally, the Ministry of Culture. Then they sent
representatives to call.

To them all, the answer was the same. 'No, the bracelet is
not for sale. No, not at any price. No, it's going back with
Rhiannon.'

To the most persistent gentleman from the Ministry the old
man said, 'You see, she'll be finding a mate overseas by and
by and then she'll be passing it on to her children or
grandchildren. So it isn't exactly hers after a manner of
speaking. It's held in trust like, isn't it? Somewhere or other
the family will go on. Just like it always have. So how can we
let you have something which belongs to generations who
haven't yet been born?'

(3)

The day following the visit from the archaeologist from the
Ministry, a registered letter was delivered to the fisherman's
cottage. It contained a restriction order signed personally by
the Minister. Its purpose was to ensure that the bracelet, a
priceless archaeological discovery, should in no circum-
stances be taken from the country. Suitable arrangements
were being made for its safe keeping and, in due course, no
more than a few weeks, he would be directed to hand it over

to whichever authority would be authorised to purchase it at a price to be laid down by the Minister.

That same evening there came to the cottage door yet another visitor. Preedy looked at him for some moments in puzzlement.

'You don't remember me,' said the man.

As soon as he spoke, Preedy laughed and held out his hand.

'Why aye, I remembers you right enough. You was the young butterfly man.'

In no time at all the kettle was boiling, the tea had been poured and Rhiannon was listening to their reminiscences.

Eventually the man said, 'I suppose you know about the road block.'

'What road block?'

'So you don't know. The police were just setting it up as I came through.'

There was only a single country lane leading from the village to the main road.

'Every vehicle is being stopped and everybody is being searched. All luggage and every parcel is being checked by a metal detector. Very thorough. You can be sure they don't mean to let your bracelet go through.'

'But they can't stop people and search 'em like that.'

'They can and will. The Minister has signed an order.'

'That'll be after that bloke who came here yesterday.'

'You recognised him, of course?'

Preedy looked puzzled.

'Me? No indeed, I've never saw him in my life before.'

The man laughed, 'He was one of those we left marooned on the rocks that day and you sent the lifeboat out to them instead. They never did forgive you for that indignity. Especially all the publicity.'

'Good God, 'tis a small world isn't it.'

'He was the archaeologist who said that you had picked up your bracelet after one of their digs over there.'

'That's nonsense.'

'I know it is.'

Preedy gave him a sharp glance.

'How d'you know 'tis nonsense?'

'Well, he was only ever a third-rater. That's why he went to the Ministry of Culture. He wouldn't have got a job anywhere else. But a close friend of mine is a professor of archaeology with a specialist interest in prehistoric and Romano British antiquities. And he said if your bracelet had been buried and subsequently dug up it would have a dark green patina. But it hasn't. The world knows that it has retained its original rich bronze lustre. Which proves your own story. So your bracelet isn't an archaeological discovery at all. It's a personal possession.'

'And what difference do that make?'

'It strengthens your argument.'

Preedy knocked his pipe out in the fireplace.

'There isn't going to be no argument.'

'What d'you mean?'

'We won't take no chances.'

The man looked at him without saying anything.

'Rhiannon and me was talkin' about this just before you come. 'Tis news about the road block but I was half expectin' somethin' of the sort.'

'So what d'you intend to do?'

Preedy was filling his pipe.

'Would you be willin' to help?' he said.

'How can I be of help?'

Again the man said nothing.

Preedy put a lighted match to his pipe, pressed the red tobacco down with the tip of a calloused finger, and when it was burning to his satisfaction, said, 'Rhiannon have never been on a French crabber and she'd enjoy that a masterpiece.'

'A French crabber?'

'There's one anchored off The Island tonight. I knows the skipper of old. I done a trip one season in his father's boat when me and him was cruts together. Tomorrow mornin' she'll be sailin' for Brittany.'

Preedy was thoughtful for a while. Then he said, 'When it comes nightfall I'll take Rhiannon out to her. The skipper can be away before dawn and I can rely on him to put her ashore on a quiet part of the English coast tomorrow night.'

He winked at the younger man. 'And I knows we can rely on you to see her safe from there to the airport.'

(4)

It had been a hard winter for the puffin. Harder than anything he had known. Not only were there the days of storm and buffeting waves, but there were the dark patches on the water which some instinct told him he must avoid. And he had seen birds dying on the water with seaweed caught fast on their legs, just as he had seen others dying caught fast in the brambles on the cliffs, and instinct now told him to avoid the rings which caused this to happen.

As in former years he felt the urge to come to The Island to find a mate, but once again he came without success. In the water there seemed to be more seals than ever and instinct again told him to be wary.

On the cliff a creature was waiting with a long rod and a noose.

The puffin flew in a wide circle round The Island. Then he headed back out to sea.

Somewhere else maybe he would one day find a mate.

(5)

Rhiannon had sailed away in the dead of night.

'You know Grandpa,' she had said before she left, 'I reckon my plane will be just about passing overhead here the day after to-morrow. So you be on the look-out and I'll wave. If the sun is shining I might even see if I can flash my bracelet for you.'

He knew that with Gaston she was in safe hands and he had never a doubt as to whether the butterfly man would play his part.

When she had gone he knew a loneliness such as he had not known since his young wife had died. Rhiannon had said she would be back next year and would be sure to have a mate. But he knew it was only her way of cheering him. Time was running out on him now.

He was leaning on his hoe in the garden in the lazy heat of the afternoon when the two men came from the Ministry of Culture. And from an important looking brief case one of them produced an important looking document. It was yet another order signed by the Ministry calling on him to hand over the bracelet in return for which he would be given a receipt. The receipt had already been made out. Nelson, the ginger cat, tail erect, stalked down the path from the cottage and jumped up to a suitable vantage point on the garden wall.

The old man looked at the document for a long time without saying anything.

'Do you understand what that says?' said the official.

'Why aye.'

'Why aye, indeed! Is that all you can ever say round here, why aye?'

'Why no.'

'Then do you understand?'

The old man did not answer. Head on one side he was listening intently. Rhiannon would find a mate and the bracelet would stay in the family.

Pointing upwards, where a great 'plane was just visible heading out to sea in the same direction as the puffin had taken, he said, 'My old eyes aren't what they used to be. Did you see something flashing in the sun?'

'Flashing?'

'Maybe you don't understand.'

'Understand what?'

'About people.'

Nelson jumped down off the wall and went back indoors.

There was a look in Preedy's eyes which would have delighted Rhiannon.